The Red Summer

Undead-Earth

The Rylie Sampson Chronicles

Book 1

First Printing, 2018

Undead-Earth.com

ISBN: 978-0-9827623-7-0

Printed in the United States of America

10 9 8 7 6 5 4 3 2 1

Contents

Chapter 1

"Come on, have a drink," Sam slurred, holding out the fortified wine.

"Never going to happen," Rylie said under her breath, ignoring the offer as she made her way by the old hobo. Nothing was free on the streets. She'd made the mistake of talking to Sam at the beginning of the summer and ever since he'd been infatuated with her. Rylie kept walking, pretending not to hear Sam describe what she was missing. For god's sake, he was old enough to be her grandfather. "Fuck off Sam", Rylie said over her shoulder as she turned the corner.

Sam watched her walk away and chuckled as she cursed at him. She might look delicate, but the girl had a mouth on her. He took a small, careful pull from the bottle, keeping his lips pressed together. It was a struggle not to tip the bottle back and pull the overly sweet wine into his mouth in gulps. The alcohol called to him, telling him to do it. Everything would be okay. Sam shook his head, arguing with himself. Nothing was free. If Sam drank the bottle too quickly he'd be hurting before nightfall for sure. The slow suffering was better than the stabbing pain and nausea that would visit him if he went a few hours without.

Sam didn't see the newcomer enter the alley until the man was right in front of him. Sam blinked, wondering what a tourist was doing so far from the safety of the street lamps and expensive stores by the waterfront. Sam smiled, pushing off the wall at the same time he started to apologize. Sam held his bottle wide as he bumped into the newcomer, chest to chest. Sam had been living on the streets for close to twenty years, and his ability to survive, to feed himself, and more importantly, to feed his alcoholism, all came down to a little bit of manual dexterity and misdirection. The man never felt the wallet being plucked from his inside jacket pocket.

"I'm so sorry," Sam mumbled as the newcomer held the old drunk at arm's length. Sam slipped the wallet into his pocket and took a sip from his bottle, keeping the newcomer's eyes where he wanted them. Even drunk Sam was a good pickpocket. "The convention center is that way," Sam said, pointing the way with his bottle.

"Show me the way," the newcomer said, his voice deep and rich, the words flowing like honey into Sam's skull. Sam nodded his head, agreeing as more words seeped into his alcohol-soaked brain. His new friend was taking him for a drink.

Time skipped for Sam. He was in the alley, and then he wasn't.

Sam lifted his bottle to his lips, but his hand was empty, his bottle was gone. He cursed himself for losing his drink, rubbing his stubbly chin as he tried to figure out where he was. It was a game he'd played many times over the years. The more he drank, the harder it was to remember the little details of life. Sam squinted against the darkness. Was it nighttime? He spun on his heel until he saw light. He shuffled towards it, his hands in front of him until they encountered something solid. Or at least he thought it was solid until his fingers slipped through the chicken wire.

Sam blinked, focusing on the two sources of light. One hung over a table that held what looked like fishing life vests, and the other was further out in the middle of whatever structure he was now in. The lightbulb in the middle of the open space cast a small circle of light on the floor. Sam had a good sense of when he was in trouble, it was a little nagging tug between his shoulders that was always a sign for him to get out of Dodge when he felt it. Sam followed the chicken wire with his hands, unable to see the floor or the walls around him. He could smell the ocean, and that meant he was somewhere near the bay. It took Sam two circuits around the ten by ten room to realize he wasn't making any progress. Two edges of the room were made from lumber and chicken wire, the other two were metal sheathing.

Sam went to the siding and felt along it, pushing until he felt a section flex under his hands. He was just beginning to push against it when a woman's scream froze him solid. He didn't want to turn around, but the scream turned into a muted cry being overridden by other, hungry sounds. He didn't want to look but there are some things you don't leave your back to.

It took Sam a long moment for his brain to organize the arms and legs on the ground, just inside the circle of light in the middle of the room. The tears came unbidden to Sam's eyes. He backed away from the chicken wire until his back was pressed to the metal siding of the warehouse, his legs shaking, unable to look away out of fear they would come closer if he took his eyes off them. Sam cried out for help, his voice joining that of at least three others he could hear but not see.

Sam pinched his eyes closed and pressed his hands to his ears, trying to blot out the reality in front of him.

It didn't work.

Chapter 2

Rylie leaned against the railing, looking out over the waters of the Pacific and the distant beaches on Coronado Island. She liked to imagine that the people who lived there had perfect lives. Every family had a doting father and a loving mother, a dog, and maybe even a cat. It was a pleasant way to pass the time.

Rylie saw the security guard out of the corner of her eye. She'd been careful not to draw any attention to herself, but security in general around San Diego had been ratcheted up. She watched as the security guard disappeared behind her, one hand slipping into her jacket pocket as she waited, not sure if she was about to get a tap on her shoulder. The trick was to move first, to make it look natural. Her hand gripped the object in her pocket, just beginning to pull it out when the security guard appeared off to her left, continuing his patrol of the marina.

Rylie let go of the object in her jacket pocket and fished around for something else. Her pockets were always full. She found her watch and pulled it free. The straps were long gone, and the screen was scratched, but it kept good time. Rylie sighed. Barely fifteen minutes had passed since the last time she'd checked.

Hunger made her inpatient, but it was still too early to go visit her connection. Instead she pushed off the railing and made her way up the walk to the hotel sitting along the water. Rylie straightened her back and lifted her chin, keeping a bored look on her face as she scanned the interior. She was the child of some rich doctor, or maybe a lawyer, someone who could easily afford a few hundred dollars to spend a night in a fancy hotel.

She belonged. It was important to believe your own lies if you wanted others to.

No one paid her any attention as she headed for the elevators and turned down a marble lined hallway. Rylie opened the door to the lady's room and smiled as it shut behind her. The bathroom was empty. She walked to the last stall and went in, locking the door behind her with a sense of excitement. The visit to the hotel bathroom was a luxury, a gift to herself. She was careful not to come into the hotel too often, but every time she did was a treat. She was in the handicap stall, and that meant there was a sink next to the toilette, the kind a wheelchair could roll under.

Rylie hung up her jacket behind the door and used the bathroom, staring at the little room that was all hers for the next twenty minutes. Unlike the stalls at fast food restaurants and gas stations, the hotel bathroom had a full-sized door. Rylie dreaded those moment in public rest rooms when your eyes met those of the person trying to open the door to the stall you were already in. It was one of the things that Rylie associated with being wealthy, nothing having to make eye contact when you were in a public rest room. Rylie stood up and smirked when the toilette flushed itself. Were rich people too lazy to flush?

Rylie wondered if rich people had self-flushing toilettes at home as she stripped down to her underwear, shivering in the overly air-conditioned air as she grabbed a paper towel from a box on the sink. They were super thick, the kind of paper towel that were meant to mimic an actual wash cloth, but still be disposable. She ran the warm water and added just a drop of soap to the towel before starting at her wrists and working her way up to her armpits, scrubbing as she went. One cloth for each arm and armpit, then another for her body and her groin. She sat back on the toilette to scrub each leg before standing to air dry. She dressed slowly, reluctant to leave the quiet solitude of her private stall for as long as possible.

When she couldn't delay any longer she stuffed a few paper towels in her pocket for later and turned to the face the stall door. She took a deep breath as her fingers rested on the latch, putting on her game face before strolling back out into the lobby. A bellboy nodded at her and received the smallest nod of acknowledgement in return. Rylie stepped briskly, pretending not to see the bellboy raise a finger, trying to get her attention. Her heart was racing as she stepped outside and slipped into the light foot traffic moving along the ocean walk.

Rylie looked relaxed, even bored. She wasn't. She was acutely aware of the time. She didn't need to check her watch anymore. The sun was edging towards the ocean. It would only be a few hours until dark.

It wasn't safe to be out after dark.

Rylie liked to be safely hiding in her bolt hole before the street lights came on. The combination of hunger and the desire to be home before dark made the decision for her. She headed back towards the convention center to see if the tradeshow traffic had died down yet. Her dinner depended on it.

Rylie shoved her hands into her jacket pocket and walked faster. She didn't have to make it all the way to the convention center. The closer she got the heavier the foot traffic became. It was a pattern she was used to. When the conventions let out for the day all the paths away from it bogged down. She turned down a side street, heading for the parking area of several nearby shops. She was going to have to wait a little longer, and she wasn't feeling super patient. She needed to do something to pass the time.

She entered the parking area as far from the shops as she could. She tried to never stay long enough in one area to be noticed, but she had a reason to come down to the Convention Center on a regular basis, and the parking lot was one of her semi regular stalking grounds. She scanned the light posts before setting down on the low wall surrounding the lot. If someone had added any cameras since her last visit they were well hidden.

Rylie reached into her jacket pocket and retrieved a smartphone. The glass was cracked, and the charging port was mangled. It wasn't important. It was just a prop. No one looked twice if you were sitting quietly and staring at your phone. Rylie watched the cars come and go from around the phone. People parked, went into the nearby shops, and then returned.

Ten minutes passed before Rylie saw the opportunity she wanted. An older blue sedan parked near the edge of the lot. Rylie walked over to the car, looked inside, and set her phone on the roof. Rylie had no interest in cars unless the owners left valuable in them. She had no idea what the differences were between a Ford and Toyota, but she knew how to spot an older model car, the kind that held no power over her primitive tools, which were in her hands in an instant, appearing smoothly from her pockets.

Her first tool was a simple wooden wedge. With nimble fingers she pulled back the weather stripping on the door and forced the wedge into place before slamming it home with a quick whack of her hand. She ignored the pain, smiling as a small gap opened at the top of the car door. Her second tool was a steel wire fastened into a small loop. A lead fishing weight was crimped onto the line just above the loop. Rylie forced this into the vehicle then scanned the parking lot. No one was paying her any attention.

She turned back to her work, telling herself she was a professional. She was sure that even professional thieves' hearts raced when they were in the middle of a heist. With practiced ease, she adjusted the wire as she lowered the snare. The locking knob stuck up, flared out, just asking to be yanked upwards. Rylie moved the wire across the top of the door, snagging the knob on the first try. She slid her end of the wire along the weather stripping until the tension on the line pulled the loop in the wire tight. The hard part was done. With a gentle tug the door unlocked.

Victory was hers.

She put her tools away and quickly climbed into the car. It was easier to run if she wasn't holding onto gear, trying not to drop it. She sat in the driver's seat and pulled the door almost closed as she scanned the interior for anything she may have missed while standing outside. The cup holder was full of loose change. She scooped up ninety percent of it and dropped it into a pocket. The real money, the paper money, was tucked above the visor. She clutched six dollars in her hand as she reached for the messenger bag in the passenger seat.

"Fuck," she cursed, setting the bag back where she'd found it. She'd hoped for a laptop or maybe a tablet, which would have gotten her twenty to fifty bucks at the pawn shop. The bag was full of worthless college textbooks. Rylie slid out of the car and shut the door. She was a block away before the owner of the car returned with a coffee and a bag of pastries. The car's owner drove away, unaware of the small act of larceny which had been visited upon her.

Rylie walked back to the waterfront, her steps light, feeling happy, enjoying the thrill of a successful heist. She sat down on a bench closer to the convention center and looked at the sun, wondering how the day could move so slow and fast at the same time.

"Assholes," she muttered to herself as she noticed the garbage sitting on the bench next to her. There was a trash can within arm's length of where she was sitting and yet the last occupant had been unable to throw their coffee cup and newspaper away.

Rylie picked up the paper, not surprised to see the headline. Another set of bodies had been found. "Asshats," Rylie said to herself, not believing what she was reading. Federal and state law enforcement agencies were arguing over how connected two separate clusters of bodies were, one in San Diego, and another in Nevada. Rylie couldn't understand why it mattered if it were one or two groups, or if it was a cult or a serial killer. Why where they investing so much time arguing over bullshit?

Rylie turned sideways on the bench and opened the paper. The left side showed a map of Nevada and a series of murders which were moving south, illustrated by a dotted line, while the other showed what was an apparently random spattering of grisly bodies found in and around San Diego.

Just under the dotted track of the Nevada murders was a box declaring that there was no known link between the events in San Diego and Nevada. The deaths in Nevada appeared to be targeting military and police while the murders in San Diego had begun with homeless people before spreading to joggers and other targets of opportunity.

Rylie traced the San Diego timeline with a finger, reading each block with morbid interest, wondering if she'd walked by the Red Summer Killer on the street. Had he thought about taking her? Rylie picked her head up and looked around, creeping herself out before going back to the paper.

The first body had been found by a sanitation worker. He saw a foot behind a dumpster and was worried he might crush someone by accident if he just went about his day. He climbed out of his truck and found he had indeed seen a foot. Just a foot. There was no body in the dumpster or anywhere nearby. This kicked off a search at the two landfills used by the city. One of the landfills turned up nothing. The relief was short lived. Nine partial bodies were found at the other. Rylie shivered as she continued to read. Two of the bodies had yet to be matched to missing people or otherwise identified. It was hard to identify a body when all you had was a forearm and part of a thigh. The bodies they did identify belonged to homeless men and women and others who lived on the fringes of society.

The second set of bodies were found within a week. A store owner called to complain about the tarp he'd seen in the undergrowth at the end of the alley behind his shop. He'd didn't need vagrants living in his alley. When the police came to investigate the loitering complaint, they found two bodies lying under the makeshift rain fly. Both were beaten so badly about their heads and shoulders that the poor victims at first appeared to have been decapitated.

Rylie heard the creak of her teeth grinding and forced herself to relax her jaw as she read. Thirty-six transients had been murdered before the public had become truly outraged. The reason the public had taken notice? Bodies thirty-seven and eight had been two joggers. The death of the joggers made the murders big news. California was experiencing its worst serial murders since the nineteen seventies when John Floyd Thomas killed at least thirty women.

Federal resources flooded into San Diego to help after the two joggers were found. The Red Summer killings were national news overnight. Rylie put her finger on the timeline, remembering those early days of summer when the murders seemed so surreal. Everyone had a theory, everyone was talking about the Red Summer Killer.

Of course, the killer went quiet. It appeared the national attention had driven him into hiding.

Rylie scrolled her finger across the timeline. A week, then two with no new bodies. Everyone thought the Red Summer Killer had fled or was lying low because of how alert law enforcement and the general population had become.

Then a woman called the police to complain about the smell coming from the apartment above hers. She thought her neighbors had graduated from being druggies to being cooks. The police kicked in the door and found a gruesome surprise. Four dismembered men inside, which turned into five when the coroner started to piece the bodies together. The corpses had been so mutilated they'd misjudged how many people were lying in the congealed pool of blood and torn flesh soaking into the carpet.

Rylie's finger moved again. It was just five days after the bodies in the apartment were found that three runners were discovered on a trail off Balboa Drive. The bodies were covered in wounds, and it didn't take long for the stories to leak to the press. It looked like the three had been forced to fight each other before they were all murdered. The level of violence and the home addresses of the three victims set the city on fire. One of three bodies found on the trail was a friend of the mayor. Rylie scanned the rest of the timeline, jumping from event to event, a shudder going down her spine as she thought about how each marker on the paper represented people's lives.

The killer struck at random. Most of the bodies belonged to the poor, the transients who endlessly moved around Sand Diego, but sprinkled in with those unfortunate souls were the bodies of the rich and wealthy who appeared to have been at the wrong place at the wrong time.

Rylie shivered in her jacket in spite of the day's warmth. The last paragraph under the San Diego story was a plea for anyone with information to call the hotline. It was clear there were no suspects, no real leads. Law enforcement was reacting to the bodies, not acting. Rylie folded the paper over on itself, so the Sand Diego story was face down. She didn't want to look at the grisly timeline any further. The Nevada killings were just as brutal, but nowhere near as numerous.

Rylie didn't understand how anyone could think the

Nevada killings were linked. The Red Summer Killer smashed his victims heads in and the bodies were all mutilated. The Nevada killings were just as brutal, but every one of them had knife wounds. The forensic analysis estimated the knife to be at least a foot long. The victims in Nevada were also very different. Soldiers, law enforcement, people in uniform were being hunted. The experts theorized it must be someone with military experience, possibly special forces. The knife work was described as distinctive.

The first Nevada body belonged to a reservist who was found in the parking lot of a bar. For all its brutality, it wasn't clear at first that it was going to be the beginning of a string of murders. The reservists body bore over thirty knife wounds. His arms had been cut so deeply at his elbows that the tendons had been severed. A week later another soldier was killed at the naval air station just over sixty miles away. He was cut down while taking out his garbage. After he was murdered his body was doused in jet fuel and set on fire. Burning the body hadn't hidden any of the knife wounds.

The police were looking for anyone with information on the nine men killed in Nevada. There was no apparent link between the dead men other than their occupations. There was a map of Nevada, showing the killings. The murderer was heading south. It wasn't a straight line, but the direction was clear. The line was tracking towards San Diego.

Ryle didn't think the killings were related. She lived on the fringes of society and knew how vulnerable that made people like herself. Whoever was hunting soldiers and cops was a different beast than the one killing homeless people and the unlucky souls caught out where their screams wouldn't carry to anyone else. For all the brutality the murders in San Diego showed, they were still going after what Rylie considered to be easy targets. She didn't think the same person was responsible for hunting soldiers, but it was still creepy as fuck.

Rylie looked up at the sky and stood quickly. She'd spent more time reading the paper than she'd realized. She threw the paper in the trash with more force than was necessary before marching off. She was going to be cutting it very close.

If the old man was still busy she was going to have to abort her mission, it was growing late and she'd be lucky to make it back to her bolt hole before the sun went down the way things were going.

Rylie felt the money in her pocket and thought about just heading back. If she didn't go to the convention center she would have enough time to grab something on the way and be safely hidden before it got truly dark. It felt wrong to spend the money so quickly though. If she used it today she was just going to be hungry again tomorrow. She walked as she argued with herself, but her feet and her stomach had already decided. She continued to the convention center.

The old man was still there, serving a lone customer who must have come out of the convention center late. The customer was large and sweating. He undid his tie as he waited, his belly sticking out from under a suit jacket that looked to have been bought when the man was a bit smaller. The big man ordered a chili cheese dog and a sprite. He wanted a cola, but he'd heard something on the news about how caffeine increased the risk of a heart attack if you had high blood pressure, so he suffered through, ordering a chili cheese dog with two slices of crispy fried bacon and drinking a Sprite because he wanted to be healthier. The old man behind the hotdog cart saw Rylie as he handed the big man his order and gave her a small wave before beginning to push his cart in her direction.

Rylie and Silvio, the old man who owned the hotdog cart, split the distance between them, meeting in the middle near a bench.

"I have six dollars," Rylie said, pulling the two bills out of her pocket. In the last year she'd eaten at least twenty of his hotdogs. She knew tourists paid four to ten dollars per dog, depending on the sides. The least she could do was offer to pay what she had.

"No, no money," Silvio said in his heavy Italian accent, waving her money away as if she had insulted him.

"Thank you," Rylie said, stuffing the bills back into her pocket. Her mouth was already watering. She didn't have to tell Silvio what she wanted. He made her one chili cheese dog and another with fried onions and dill relish before making himself a plain dog. His homemade chili called to him, but the evening of heart burn wasn't worth the few moments of pleasure the chili would bring to him. He grabbed two sodas at random and put them down next to Rylie on the bench before sitting down at the opposite end.

Silvio was always careful to move slowly around her. It hurt him to see how closely she watched him, still afraid that his kindness was a mask for some other motive. Silvio didn't have a daughter but it pained him to see the wariness in her. She was so young to hold so much fear in her.

"Maybe you want a job?" Silvio asked after chewing and swallowing two bites of his hot dog, the words slipping out of his mouth. He'd thought about saying them many times, but was afraid. Afraid she'd think he wanted cheap labor, afraid she'd do something stupid and he would cause trouble for whichever friend agreed to hire her. He looked over at her, relieved to see her hesitation was caused by a mouthful of food and nothing else. She held up a finger as she sipped her soda, swallowing the last bite of hotdog number one. She'd been very hungry.

"Eleven months," Rylie said the moment her mouth was clear.

"Eleven months?" Silvio asked, not quite understanding.

"In eleven months I'll be an adult as far as the state is concerned. Until then I can't risk getting drug back into the system," she said apologetically. When she turned eighteen she would be a legal adult. Until then she didn't have a lot of options. After her mother passed away she'd bounced around foster homes and then the state-run school for troubled children. At least they called it a school, it was more of a mental hospital than an educational facility. She'd rather live on the streets.

"I will talk to my friends, and when it is time you'll have a job," the old man said, nodding his head. He would start with his friend Anthony. Anthony's family business was catering, and they were always looking for staff. "Family?" Silvio asked carefully. He'd fed her all summer, and while Rylie was a quiet one, Silvio was a talker. It was hard for him not ask her too many questions.

"Hmm," Rylie said, taking her time chewing her first bite of her onion and relish dog. She stared at the ground between her feet intently, a small war raging in her skull. She didn't want to think about her past but neither did she want to be rude. As sad as it was, Silvio was the closest thing she had to a friend. The first time he'd given her a hotdog he'd just walked by and handed it to her before walking away, his cart never slowing. To her it had been completely random. To him it was a small gesture of kindness after watching the skinny girl staring at his cart on and off all afternoon. A week later when hunger had driven her back to where she'd first seen the old man by the convention center she'd received a dog and a soda. The fact that he did it quietly, without a word between them was what kept her coming back in those early days.

Rylie looked over at him. His hair was white and sparse and his skin was wrinkled and covered in liver spots. He was looking down nervously, afraid he'd broken whatever unsaid agreement existed between them. She swallowed the lump in her throat and spoke. "My mother was white. My father was black. Her family disowned her when she married him. He died when I was very young, I never knew him" she said, her voice hollow and soft. "My mom died four years ago. If I have any family, I don't know who they are." The words burnt her throat as she said them.

Rylie told herself she was a loner, she was tough. She had armor that nothing could pierce. Armor just didn't help when the pain was coming from the inside. She missed her mother.

"I'm sorry," Silvio said, fighting back the urge to reach out and grip her shoulder. He could see the pain in her, see how hard she fought not to let it show.

"Did you think I was Italian?" she said quickly, changing

the subject, smiling a little as she looked over at him.

"Ha," he shrugged, then smiled. "A little," he admitted.

"It's okay," she said, smiling back. One of the gifts of her mixed race was that she looked a little bit like everyone. Her skin tone was dark enough to make her look mildly exotic but also let her pass for about any ethnic group she wanted to blend in with.

They finished eating in peaceful silence.

"You be safe," Silvio said earnestly, wishing his words had power over the world to make them real. He dusted crumbs from his lap and used the edge of the cart to help himself get off the bench. He wanted to say something more, to make sure she had someplace to go. His fear of scaring her off kept him quiet, but at the same time he felt like he was racing against every other horrible thing the streets could bring to bear. He was an old man, he wasn't sure if he had eleven more months, or even eleven days left. Other than painful arthritis he was healthy as far as he knew, but he was also at an age where he'd seen many of his friends die. One day they were playing pinochle together, the next day he'd find out they were gone. He didn't want to miss the chance to do this one last kindness in the world and help her off the streets. He decided he'd just have to live for eleven more months no matter what.

Rylie thanked him again, standing as she finished her soda. She stretched, feeling sluggish now that her belly was full. If she'd closed her eyes she would have fallen asleep standing up. It took an effort to make her legs move.

Her spirits were high as she walked. The gnawing hunger she'd suffered with all morning was finally at rest, put off for at least a few hours, and she had cash in her pocket. Overall it was a good day. Even with a belly full of hotdogs and soda Rylie's feet floated over the pavement.

Rylie moved through the foot traffic around the convention center easily, slowly making her way back to her bolt hole with a sense of light heartedness. The positive vibes lasted until she caught her toe on an uneven bit of pavement and had to catch her balance, barely avoiding eating some concrete. "Fuck," Rylie muttered with a laugh, glad she'd been able to stay on her feet. She took two more steps before the first raindrop hit her. She looked up and cursed again, this time without any mirth. The sky overhead was growing prematurely dark with storm clouds. She picked up her pace, imagining that she could step between the raindrops as they fell randomly around her. She desperately hoped the rain would hold off a little longer, but she knew it was a slim chance. The air was heavy with the scent of the coming storm. She was about to get wet. It made her wish she could have hidden back near the waterfront, but there was too much security there. The moment you appeared to be something other than a tourist or a local out for a walk they would be all over you.

Rylie picked up her pace until her calves were burning. She would have jogged if it meant getting back to her bolt hole before the skies opened up, but she still had a twenty-minute walk in front of her and the rain was already picking up, turning from sporadic drops to a slow steady downfall. She rubbed her food baby as she walked, telling the hotdogs in her stomach they had been worth it.

"Choices, choices," Rylie muttered as she came to a critical juncture. She was only halfway to her bolt hole and had to decide which path to finish the journey. She pulled her hood over her head and held out her hand, watching the rain strike her palm as she thought.

The quick or the short path?

The quicker path cut through an industrial park along the waterfront, the longer way kept her under streetlamps for a good bit of the way, but she would be completely soaked by the time she got to her bolt hole. She stopped at the corner where she would need to decide, glancing at the two paths in front of her. She looked at the buildings along the waterfront and the way they were already casting long dark shadows on the road. The longer she watched the more the dark seemed liquid, moving between and around the buildings. She imagined she could see movement there, creeping herself out.

"God damn it," she mumbled, she hated feeling afraid. She told herself the cold running down her spine was just the rain. She was ashamed of that fear, and it only made her more frustrated that she was unable to decide, standing there for everyone to see as she struggled with the decision. You never knew when someone was watching you, sizing you up. Even before the Red Summer had begun, you never wanted to look weak.

The weak were prey.

The strong took from the weak. Sometimes it was food, sometimes it was money if you had any, and sometimes it was worse. Rylie shook her head, pushing the dark thoughts away. The rain picked up, becoming a light but steady downfall.

She looked up into the falling rain and turned towards the street lamps, resigning herself to a long, wet night. She was going to be soaked no matter what path she took so it didn't really matter. Or at least that is what she told herself as she tucked her hands into her pockets and turned away from the shorter path. A few cars came and went, rolling by as she trudged onward. She made it three blocks before she encountered a young man coming the opposite way.

The young man's shoulders and body were rolled forward, his ball cap tilted down to try and shield his eyes from the rain. He jumped when he saw Rylie's feet come into view, not expecting to see anyone else stuck out in the rain. The way he stiffened as he approached made Rylie's heart race. She took one hand out of her pocket, her fist a tight little ball as their paths brought them shoulder to shoulder.

Rylie was ready to turn and swing – to get one shot in before she bolted.

The stranger continued to walk, never realizing how close he'd come to getting punched in the side of the head by a nervous girl passing him in the rain. Rylie sighed, letting her balled fist relax as she continued to walk, the adrenaline flowing through her veins making her feel shaky.

"Fuck, fuck, fuck," Rylie chanted under her breath. She'd just wanted a hotdog, but now she was soaking wet, cold, and pissed at herself. It was going to take days to get completely dry. The rain was squishing in her shoes and her jacket, which wasn't waterproof, was starting to get heavy with moisture.

She'd been able to steer clear of trouble for over a year by following a simple set of rules. No run ins with the police or social services. No fights over where she was squatting or the best places to hustle. It was better to move along than to start wars. Many of the people she rubbed shoulders with were less than stable, so she followed her rules and stayed out of trouble. At the start of the Red Summer she'd implemented a new rule.

Don't stay out after dark.

She berated herself as she walked. She should have just left and spent the money she'd boosted instead of waiting for a hotdog. She'd seen the clouds in the distance. The rain and the shadowy pre-dusk should not have been a surprise. If she'd listened to something other than her stomach at least.

Rylie let the cold rain soak into her. It was an acceptable punishment for letting herself be caught out in the dark and the rain. She had no one to blame but herself. She'd broken the summers most important rule. Be home before dark.

The small ball of anxiety in her belly was blossoming. Every noise sounded like a footfall behind her and the rain was picking up, making her squint to see more than a few dozen feet in front of her. If there was one thing that her life had taught her, it was that breaking rules had consequences.

She wasn't religious, but it didn't keep her from bargaining with whatever powers might have been listening to her thoughts. She had learned her lesson. She'd never break any of her rules again. She'd be hiding in her little box of a living space an hour before dusk – no exceptions. If Silvio had a line she'd wave and try again the next day. A few hot dogs were not worth getting caught out after dark in the rain. The full stomach she'd been so happy to have a half hour before had now turned sour and heavy in her gut.

Chapter 3

Sam wasn't quite sure what was real and what wasn't anymore. He'd watched a man attack and brutally murder a woman who was begging for mercy. She seemed to have known the man attacking her. Sam shook his head, trying to drive the memory out of his skull.

He didn't feel well, but fear kept him moving. He looked over his shoulder, making sure no one was following him. He'd been pushed out onto the floor of the warehouse with several others. Two of those others weren't right. The thought made him look down at this hand. The woman had barely gotten her teeth into him, but his hand pulsed with pain, the heat already burning a path from the wound up to his shoulder.

Sam knew he'd gotten lucky. Several of the others had tried to fight. It had given him the split second to run. He found the metal wall of the warehouse and found the bottom had been rusted out. Panic and fear had given him the strength to push his way under.

He needed to get back to his bolt hole, find a bottle, and hide until he felt better.

Chapter 4

Rylie was alternating between berating herself and promising herself she was going to steal an umbrella the first chance she got as the rain sucked the heat from her body, making her fingers and toes numb with cold. She was on the final stretch, just three blocks and she'd be able to climb onto the roof of the defunct garage where she'd built a small living space out of what had been a massive air handler. She was distracted, thinking about peeling off her cold, wet clothes and hiding under the blankets she horded to keep warm against the cool nighttime air. When she saw Sam stumble onto the street in front of her she wasn't even upset. It was just one more shitty thing to cap off a shitty night.

Rylie was almost relieved to see how the hobo was swaying on his feet. He was so drunk he could barely walk. A car sped by along the street, momentarily blinding Rylie with its headlights. She blinked away the stars in her eyes as she continued to close on Sam.

"Fuck off, it's already been a long day," Rylie said casually, rain spraying off her lips as she cursed. The old man didn't react. He continued to walk drunkenly her way. The rain dripped off his face and turned the old beaten up suite he wore dark. If he wasn't so clearly impaired the rain might have made him look like an executive who had gotten caught out in the weather.

Rylie tried to go wide around the old man. He moved to match her on the sidewalk, blocking her way. Rylie felt her face flush as fear and anxiety turned quickly to anger and frustration. She wasn't in the mood to deal with the old man's shit tonight.

She squared her shoulders and jabbed a finger in his direction as he took several small steps her way, closing the final distance between them.

"You are going to leave me alone," Rylie demanded, her voice loud and sharp. Sam ignored her, his feet dragging as he took the last step towards her. "Fuck off," she barked, wondering if he was sober enough to even understand her. He barely shifted his gaze to look at her as she spoke.

"Fucking drunk," Rylie grumbled in resignation, pushing his shoulder away from her as she moved past him, refusing to step around him again. Rylie had a brief feeling of self-satisfaction for dealing with Sam so directly. It lasted until his hand fell on her shoulder. She cursed as she spun around, trying to shrug his hand free, an epic rant forming on her lips. She blinked away the rain, the words dying on her lips as she came face to face with Sam.

His face was hollow and sunken and there was something wrong with his eyes. His pupils were massive dark circles rimmed with bright red blood. What the hell had the old hobo been drinking? Rylie sincerely hoped it wasn't the bath salts that made you want to eat someone's face.

"Let go," Rylie screeched, her voice high and shrill with a mix of anger and surprise. As frail as the old man looked his grip was steel. His fingers tightened, wrapping around the meat of her shoulder. Rylie screamed, her anger evaporating as the pain in her shoulder turned it to fear. She looked up and down the street, hoping to see someone, anyone who could help. There were vehicles stopped at the corner, waiting for the light to change, but the sidewalk was empty of other pedestrians.

"No," she screamed, slamming both her hands into Sam's chest. He stumbled, pulling her with him as his grip continued to tighten painfully. Rylie's scream turned shrill as the old hobo's fingers dug into her flesh. Rylie took a panting breath, the rain hiding the tears streaming down her face. She fought back the urge to scream and flail and instead focused on her attacker's wrist, slamming both her hands into it.

Each time she struck the hobo's wrist his fingers tore at her shoulder blade, but she didn't stop. She howled in pain and frustration as she put everything she had into freeing herself, desperately trying to break his grip. Her shoulder was on fire, it felt like his fingers and thumb were about to join around her collar bone.

Rylie never saw Sam's other arm coming, she was too focused on trying to free herself. The blow hit her on the side of the head with enough force to stun her. She clutched at the Sam's chest, grabbing a handful of his jacket to hold herself up, trying to save herself from the pain in her shoulder as her body weight dangled from his grip.

"What's wrong with you?" Rylie screamed, kicking him as best she could, trying to find the soft spot between his legs. Pain turned to panic, she had to get away. She pounded at his chest, kicking and kneeing with little effect as Sam pulled her closer, wrapping his free arm around her. "No," she begged as he crushed her against his body, pushing the air from her lungs.

The thin line that had been the hobo's lips parted and his mouth slowly opened. Rylie threw her head back, trying to get away from his mouth. Rylie fought, squirming and writhing, trying to get away, but Sam was so strong and nothing she did seemed to have any effect. She sucked in a little breath, pulled back her knee, and drove it into the hobo where she thought his balls should be. Her knee made solid contact, striking with enough force to drop anyone who wasn't numb to the world.

Sam didn't seem to feel the blow at all.

Rylie felt the grip on her shoulder release and she had a brief moment of elation, maybe Sam was just so drunk it took a moment for the blow to register? The spike of relief lasted only a moment. Sam wasn't letting her go, he was shifting his grip, wrapping both arms around her. He pulled her tight with a sharp jerk, bringing them face to face as a low grumble escaped his lips. Rylie gagged, trying unsuccessfully to shrink away from the smell of liquid garbage washing over her.

Rylie kicked her legs, her scream cut short as Sam worked his arms around her, his grip tightening like a snake as he hugged her tighter and tighter. Rylie filled her lungs against the external pressure, trying to take small breaths while keeping her lungs inflated against the squeezing force of Sam's arms. Rylie concentrated on breathing, fighting back the urge to scream again, which she knew would cost her the last air she had in her lungs. Sam's mouth was on her neck before she could do anything. She twisted her head, trying to keep his mouth off her flesh as his jaws opened and closed with a wet smacking sound. His grip tightened, forcing the air out of lungs in a long hiss as she tried to use her head as a battering ram.

"No," Rylie begged, the rain and her tears sliding down her cheeks as Sam's mouth formed a cold circle of pressure on her neck. His grip was too tight, his strength too great. Ryle's chest burnt under the pressure of his arms.

Everything was fading. Rylie desperately needed to breathe. The cold circle at her neck intensified as the Hobo sucked, pulling her skin into his mouth. She wanted to pull away, she wanted to do something, anything, but was helpless as he bit down. Fresh pain flowed. The Hobo worked his jaws, grinding away at Rylie's flesh. The pain was a bright light in a room growing dark. Rylie embraced it, held onto the pain against the rising tide of unconsciousness, the deep, primal part of her brain whispering that passing out meant death.

Rylie's vision was narrowing and the pressure on her chest was slowly forcing the air out of her lungs. The small kernel of her brain which was still functioning was panicked and at peace at the same time. The pain was moving further away. Dying sucked, but it was not as bad as she feared. The last of the air in her lungs was pressed from her and she found her body unable to pull more in. Her mouth was open, but her ribs were being crushed. Rylie lifted her head to the rain, no longer fighting. Unconscious, death, it didn't matter anymore.

The end was not what Rylie expected. There was a violent jerk. She wondered if that was her soul leaving her body as she pulled in a deep breath, the air tasted clean and salty as she was jerked about again.

"Uhhh," Rylie groaned, the sound of her own voice centering her a little as she continued to pull air into her lungs in deep breaths. She wasn't quite dead yet after all. She pulled air in desperately as the world shifted violently around her again. The sudden movement made the hot dogs in her belly rise in her throat. She swallowed them down, forcing herself not to vomit. Breathing was more important. She sucked in long breaths and blew them out until she was coughing, her ribs on fire as they expanded and contracted, free of the crushing pressure that had bound them. Rylie blinked, shaking her head. Her legs felt weak and rubbery. It wasn't until her eyes focused on Sam that she realized she wasn't free yet. One of Sam's hands gripped the front of her sweatshirt in a ball, holding her weight as her legs dangled in a rubbery mass beneath her.

"Run," someone screamed. Rylie's feet moved beneath her, dragging over the wet concrete as Sam held her in place. She was trying, she just wasn't getting anywhere. "Run," the voice urged again, and Rylie nodded, trying to shake off the cloud of haze around her thoughts.

Rylie concentrated her feet, on taking the weight of her body onto her legs until she found her footing, her legs holding her up, so she was no longer hanging from the Sam's fist. She leaned back, grunting as she tried to pull her sweatshirt from Sam's grip.

She'd never been so happy to see another person in her life. She wasn't alone against Sam anymore. Someone else was there. A young man in jeans was standing off to her side, his body twisting as he put everything he had into a massive right hook. The punch landed hard, forcing Sam to take two shuffling steps to keep his feet under him. If it weren't for his grip on Rylie's clothing he would have fallen. Instead she was pulled along behind him as he stumbled, counterbalancing him and keeping him upright in the process.

The Good Samaritan was right there, grabbing the fabric of Rylie's shirt and pulling, adding his strength to hers as they both fought to break Sam's grip. The Good Samaritan's shift in focus was a mistake. Sam brought his left arm around like a battering ram, catching the young man on his shoulder with a clumsy but powerful blow. The Good Samaritan stumbled but kept his feet, a look of surprise and anger on his face as he put his hands up in front of himself, ready to fight.

"Call nine-one-one," a woman screamed from where she'd stopped, about to get into her car. Rylie nodded her head, agreeing that it might be time for a few cops to show up. The woman stood behind her car, hiding under her umbrella as she watched the fight, screaming for someone to call for help. She'd left her cell phone at home.

"Call this freak an ambulance," the young man said to himself, his stance changing as he squared his shoulders and put his fists in front of his face in a classic boxer's pose. He stepped forward, moving from side to side, his head and upper body in constant motion. It would have looked sad or comical as he stepped within punching distance of Sam if you hadn't seen the hobo take two blows that should have already dropped him. Sam reacted slowly, his head coming around to look at the Good Samaritan just in time to receive two quick jabs. The blows left Sam's nose clearly broken, fresh dark blood oozing down over his mouth.

"Let her go," the Good Samaritan demanded. Sam didn't respond. His facial expression barely changed. The Good Samaritan struck two more quick blows and stepped back, his brow furrowing. Sam's face was a mask of split skin, and dark streaks where the rain was washing blood away, but the hobo was still on his feet, and the Good Samaritan wasn't pulling any punches.

"Come on," the Good Samaritan said under his breath, moving from side to side, ready to attack again. Sam turned to Rylie and made a growl low in his chest, his garbage breath washing over her as he snarled, his mouth a gaping maw. Rylie was struck with the nervous urge to giggle. Sam was all lips and gums. If her ribs weren't on fire she would have laughed. It's hard to eat someone's face without any teeth. The thought struck Rylie as hugely funny. Then it scared her. She wasn't sure if she was in shock.

With a jerky movement of his fingers Sam let go of Rylie's clothing and turned to face the Good Samaritan. Rylie staggered backwards, almost overbalancing as the counterweight she'd been pulling against was removed. Sam growled again, the sound deep and low as he faced off with the Good Samaritan.

Sam and the Good Samaritan stood across from each other, the rain dancing at their feet as they faced off.

The Good Samaritan was in constant motion, his weight moving from foot to foot on the balls of his feet. He breathed rhythmically as he moved from side to side, his body ready to dodge punches as if Sam were going to turn into a boxer at any moment. Sam stood completely still, staring at his opponent with unnatural calm.

From a distance, it looked like a young thug attacking an old man. The Good Samaritan was a gym boxer, not a professional by any means, but he looked like a pro as he threw a combination, his right fist, then his left striking Sam in rapid succession. Sam took the blows, his head knocked back until his bloodshot eyes were staring up into the light of the nearest street lamp. It didn't slow Sam down. He reached out his hands and stepped forward as he began to bring his head down. The Good Samaritan moved between Sam's outstretched arms, trying to land a massive undercut just as the old man was bringing his chin down.

The Good Samaritan didn't realize the danger he was in. He tried to brush one of Sam's arms away, to get inside the older man's reach to land what he hoped would be the knockout punch. Instead the Good Samaritan found Sam's arm to be an iron bar, and instead of brushing it aside, he simply put his own left arm directly into Sam's grip. Sam used that handhold to yank the younger man forward, grabbing the Good Samaritan's arm in both hands.

The Good Samaritan tied to throw a punch with his free arm, but Sam took all the fight out him when he snapped the younger man's arm like a tree branch. The Good Samaritan screamed, high and shrill, his eyes locked on the white of the bone sticking out from just above his left elbow.

At the beginning of the summer Rylie had seen a sleeping dog get its tail rolled over by one of the electric carts they used on the pier to haul trash. One moment there had been quiet, and then the dog was howling, the sound full of shock and pain. The heavy cart had cut half the dogs tail clean off. The dog couldn't comprehend how it had been hurt so badly and so quickly. The sound coming from the Good Samaritan reminded Rylie of that moment.

Sam let go of the Good Samaritan who promptly fell to the ground. As he fell his lower arm flopped, bringing forth fresh screams of agony. Sam ignored the cries, looking one way, then the other until he found Rylie.

Rylie stood, unable to look away from Sam and the young man who had tried to help her. She was frozen, her brain overloaded by the craziness of what she was experiencing. She knew she should do something, she should try and help the young man, she should run, she should attack. The thoughts rushed through her head over and over in an endless loop, holding her in place.

Sirens switched on close by. The police car had been just two blocks away when the call came in from dispatch. The sound cut through the Good Samaritan's screams and Rylie's hesitation at the same time. She blinked, looked at Sam, and spun on her heel, her instincts taking over where her mind had failed her. Her instincts knew to run. She let her primal instincts take over, it was time to flee.

Rylie made it across the first lane of traffic before she heard the woman hiding behind her car screaming, "Watch out!" She turned just in time to see Sam charging in an odd, ungainly run. He hit her full in the chest, carrying her off her feet. Rylie had an odd thought as she felt Sam wrap his arms around her. Why was the woman still screaming, "Watch out?"

Rylie found out a moment later when the bus hit them.

The bus hit Sam first, driving him into Rylie with enough force to pick her up off her feet. Sam's head slammed back into the flat windshield, sending an explosion of cracks through the glass. Both their bodies were pinned to the front of the vehicle for a split second until the driver slammed on the brakes. Then world spun around Rylie in a kaleidoscope of colors and confusing images as she tensed, waiting for the pain. Her feet scraped across the pavement, then her butt hit, sending her upper body backwards to tumble end over end. Sam was less lucky. He slid off the front of the bus and under the left front tires, parts of him spraying over the street in a wet, chunky explosion. The wallet he'd stolen earlier that day went flying before slipping between the grates of a storm drain and falling into the streaming water below.

Rylie was dimly aware of coming to a stop. She couldn't remember why she was in the shower – or why there was no hot water. She slipped off into unconsciousness trying to remember why she should be alarmed.

Chapter 5

Rylie had a headache. For a long time, it was the only thing she was aware of. She felt like someone had replaced her brain with a bag of broken glass and rocks. One moment she felt stabbing pain that bounced around the back of her skull and then dull aches that seemed to reach into her eye sockets.

She also had to pee.

The realization that her bladder was full made the headache even worse. Somehow the combination of the two discomforts greatly outweighed what either of them should have been alone.

She tried to open her eyes and quickly regretted it. The light slipping by her eyelids formed spears of fire that bounced around behind her eyes. For three heavy breaths, she forgot about her bladder. She lay there, contemplating her current situation, trying to remember where she was and how she'd gotten there. Only, she couldn't really remember, which worried her. The worry drove her to open her eyes once more, this time much more carefully. She eased her eyes open slowly, opening them to narrow slits. She needed to see where she was. The realization that she didn't know such a simple fact set her heart on a little race. Hadn't she been thinking about the Red Summer? She felt like something bad had happened, she just couldn't remember what.

She wanted to clamp her eyes shut and ignore the anxiety slowly building inside of her. Instead she forced herself to open her eyes a little bit more. Tendrils of pain slipped through, forming a tight ball of pressure just behind her eyes. It hurt, but it was bearable. Each time the pain would ebb she opened her eyes further, letting them adjust to the light before doing it again. She had no idea where she was. Rylie just needed to see a glimpse of her surroundings to orient herself. To reassure herself.

It was a long moment of staring at brightness before Rylie realized she had her eyes open, but all she could see was light. Anxiety blossomed. She couldn't get her eyes to focus. She blinked slowly, mildly relieved when her view changed from light to dark. She wasn't blind, or at least not completely blind. She tried to think about what had happened, but it was hard to remember. Her mind was randomly shifting from one thought to the next. She couldn't concentrate. She closed her eyes to try and think and found herself floating on the edge of sleep, drifting off, then waking up as pain and her full bladder reminded her she wasn't going to rest easily.

She sleepily thought that closing her eyes had been counterproductive.

It was her bladder more than the pain which finally brought her out of her stupor. She was going to have to pee soon, one way or the other. She opened her eyes slowly again, it didn't take as long for them to adjust to the light this time, and held them open until she had to blink. The pain Rylie felt was sharper and less focused at the same time. She felt more aware. Her world was no longer her headache and her bladder. She stretched her fingers out, feeling the mattress under her. As she breathed she could feel the sheet what was covering her up to her neck.

She blinked, watching as her view went light then dark. As she did so she realized she could feel something brushing against her lashes. She smiled happily to herself. Something was wrapped around her head, obscuring her vision. Maybe she wasn't blind after all. Being more aware had its draw back as well though. She not only had to pee, she hurt from the top of her head down to her knees and each body part that hurt was trying to convince her it was the most injured. Rylie smiled to herself anyway. She was pretty sure she knew where she was.

She didn't know how she'd gotten there, the last few hours were a haze, but the crisp sheets and the smell, it meant she must have had an accident. She was in a hospital. She'd get herself patched up and slip off the first chance she got. The thought made her smile at herself. She had a plan, and that helped push the anxiety away.

The sound of something moving nearby wiped the smile off her face. She clamped her eyes closed and went very still. Someone was talking. No, two people. There were two people in the room with her. They talked in hushed voices, just loud enough that she could hear them without understanding what they were saying.

She was about to ask for help when the thought triggered a memory.

Help. It is such a simple and loaded word.

Bits and pieces of the night before came back to her in a rush. She remembered walking in the rain. Images flashed by, little bits of disjointed memories washing over her in a flood. It was dark, Sam grabbed her, and then the Good Samaritan was looking at his broken arm. She remembered being afraid.

Something had been very wrong with Sam. She involuntarily relived the moment the bus hit them and shivered.

It was an effort not to let panic take control. She forced herself to stay calm, to think about the here and now. She could feel the mattress under her. She wasn't on the street anymore. She inhaled through her nose until a jab of pain warned her against filling her lungs too fully. She was in the hospital. Hospitals were safe.

Something beeped softly then whirred off to her left.

She concentrated on the sound, trying to understand what was making the noise as a pleasant warmth flushed through her. She took another deep breath and the pain in her ribs was different. Instead of the sharp stabbing it had been a moment before it was distant and dull. She took several more breathes, her body floating in a warm haze of comfort. At least until her nose started to itch, pulling her out of her pleasant stupor. She reached up with her hand, her fingers moving to scratch her nose.

She could feel her fingers moving but the itch wouldn't go away. She rubbed her thumb and forefinger together and smiled at herself when she realized her hand wasn't anywhere near her nose. The smile fell off her face when someone else in the room laughed softly. She was being watched. Rylie hated being laughed at. She lifted her right hand to give her observer the finger only to have it stopped short with a metallic click at the same time metal bit into her wrist. The soft laughter turned into a belly laugh. Rylie could only keep track of a single thought at a time. She moved her hand, trying to understand what was restricting her wrist from moving freely. She tugged against it, listening to the gentle metallic noise as the handcuff slid along the bed frame.

"Fug yoo," Rylie murmured, her dry lips and the sedation making her barely understandable. She licked her lips and discovered her tongue wasn't much help, which made her realize how thirsty she was. How could her mouth by so dry when her bladder was filled to bursting? The thought made her smile.

She lifted her left hand and felt something pull gently at that wrist as well. She felt around blindly, expecting to find another handcuff. Instead there was a tangle of soft tubing. It took Rylie's muddled brain several more moments of contemplation to realize she was touching her intravenous line. It was a relief of sorts, being handcuffed twice seemed, well, twice as bad as being handcuffed once.

Rylie felt around with her left hand, dragging the IV tubing behind her. She found the edge of the sheet and pulled it tighter, sliding her right hand and the handcuff around her wrist back under the covers. There was just enough length to the cuffs that she could rest her right hand on her stomach. She grabbed the cold metal of the cuff with her left hand and pulled. First gently, then harder, trying to slip her hand free.

The belly laugh from next to her was louder this time. Rylie wasn't being as sneaky as she thought. It didn't matter; whoever had cuffed her had used a pair of small cuffs. Her petite frame wasn't going to save her.

She put her hands back on top of the covers.

"Yeah, I hope it isn't too tight," a gruff male voice said, clearly amused.

"Fucking donut eater," she mumbled, the words slurring in her mouth. The man's laugher died as soon as she spoke, which told her the man in her room was indeed a cop. She knew that was bad, she just had to remember why. The painkillers were making it hard to think.

"Want me to pinch off your morphine?" the man asked. He sounded like he was only half joking. The light on the left side of the bed grew dim as someone stepped closer.

"Yes, I don't like drugs," Rylie said with a smile, trying not to giggle.

"I bet," the man said, judging Rylie on the goofy smile on her face and not the words she'd spoken.

"Fucking cops," she said, relaxing back into her pillow. She felt the bed move as the cop wrapped his hands around the bed rail, squeezing until two of his knuckles popped. The smile faltered on Rylie's face. She tried to lay very still, as if that would keep the cop from doing anything. She normally didn't make mistakes like pissing off people bigger than her – but at the same time she wasn't normally drugged and blind to any visual cues of what the other person was thinking either.

"Okay officer, that's enough," a woman said. There was something in her tone that brooked no argument. The new voice expected to be obeyed. "Out in the hallway," she commanded. There was sound and movement and a transition of shadows as someone else stepped up to the bed. Rylie jumped when a hand touched her forehead, easing the gauze away from her eyes. She squinted up, relieved to be able to see, even if the overhead light was still too bright.

"I have to pee," Rylie begged.

"I'll call for some help," the woman said, her hand falling to Rylie's shoulder as she spoke. Rylie's arm twitched under the touch as she blinked away the cobwebs in her eyes. "You're safe here, no one will hurt you," the woman promised; her tone soft and soothing. She reached over Rylie to pull a cord behind the bed, turning out the brightest of the lights.

"Please, I really have to go," Rylie begged, trying to sound desperate, which was not so far from the truth.

"You going to give me any trouble?" the woman asked, her eyebrows bunching up skeptically as she looked over her charge.

"I think walking will be enough of a challenge. Please?" Rylie begged, crossing her legs under the sheets for dramatic effect.

The woman paused, clearly thinking through her decision before answering. "Okay," she agreed, walking around the bed so she could pull the IV pole into a better position. Rylie tried not to let the excitement show on her face as the woman grabbed her wrist. Warm fingers held her arm in place as the cuffs were unlocked. Rylie flexed her toes as the woman let down the guardrails on her right.

"Sit up slowly," the woman said, taking Rylie's hand to help her sit.

Rylie twisted as she sat up, letting her legs slide over the edge of the bed, no longer as excited as she'd been just thirty seconds before. With the cuffs off and just the young woman in her room she'd thought she'd have a chance to make some type of escape. It was a short-lived plan. Sitting up was an effort that made the pain in her skull and ribs burn through the meds. She sat on the edge of the bed, panting, sweat breaking out on her skin that quickly turned to a chill in the overly air-conditioned room.

"You want to lie back down? I can get a bedpan brought in," the woman said, looking at Rylie skeptically.

"Just needed a second to orient myself," Rylie said. It hurt to breath.

"How about we compromise," the woman said, keeping one hand on Rylie to make sure she didn't' fall forward as she used her foot to pull a commode chair closer.

"I really have to pee," Rylie said through gritted teeth, shifting her weight forward until her feet slapped gently down onto the cold floor. The woman was immediately next to her, wrapping an arm around Rylie's upper body to help support her.

"Please don't fall, just let me spin you about and I'll help you to sit down," the woman said, clearly alarmed now that Rylie's wellbeing was literally in her hands.

Rylie was so drowsy she didn't even care that her ass was hanging out the back of her hospital gown as she stood up. Her helper turned her and slowly lowered her down onto the commode chair. It hurt to sit down, even with the woman supporting a good bit of her weight. Rylie hissed when her naked butt hit the icy plastic of the commode.

"You okay?" the woman asked, a little alarmed.

"Just freezing," Rylie mumbled. She shut her eyes and peed, no longer able to hold it now that her body knew she was sitting on a commode. Normally she wouldn't have been able to pee with someone else in the room with her. Desperate times call for desperate measures however. Keeping her eyes shut helped. She relaxed, her shoulders rolling forward as she was filled with relief that temporarily blotted out everything else. As she peed she felt along the IV tubing. A few inches up she found the little plastic clamp she was looking for and pinched it closed.

"You sure you want to do that?" the woman asked. Rylie opened her eyes and followed the sound of the woman's voice to where she was leaning against the end of the bed. The other woman's eyes were locked on Rylie's.

"I don't like drugs," Rylie said, repeating herself, taking a good long look at the other woman. She'd assumed her helper was a nurse at first, but she had been more interested in peeing than anything else at the time. Rylie scanned her helper, trying to pin down just what she was dealing with. The other woman was just an inch or two taller than herself, so she was also on the petite side, but where Rylie looked like a strong gust of wind could carry her into the air, her helper looked like she could do a hundred pull ups without breaking a sweat. She had a compact physicality about her that matched the air of self-confidence the woman carried herself with perfectly. Rylie looked over the woman's clothing, but the dark slacks and blazer didn't give her any more information. The clothing was decent but could have been bought by anyone from a nurse administrator to a corporate executive.

Rylie looked at her fingers as she continued to pee. She had some small cuts and abrasions but neither hand showed any evidence of fingerprint ink. Rylie hoped that meant they didn't know who she was. She didn't carry any identification. Not seeing any purple ink on her hands made Rylie feel better. It didn't really matter who the woman in front of her was as her own identify was still a secret.

The thought of being identified made Rylie shiver from more than just the ice-cold plastic her butt was sitting on. The idea of being found made her wonder if she could she overpower her helper and escape? Rylie thought about it for a moment before sighing heavily. In her current state she wasn't sure she could overpower a kitten.

Reality was a bitch.

"Not liking drugs seems like a good thing, but these were prescribed by a doctor," the woman said, bringing Rylie's attention back to her helper.

"My father was an addict, I don't like drugs," Rylie said. She was still peeing. It felt weird to be talking to a stranger as she relieved herself. She'd never done the whole group bathroom thing like other girls.

"Was?" the woman asked. Rylie nodded and cut off what she was going to say. Social worker, definitely a social worker Rylie thought. It was the way the woman talked. Easy, confident, it made you want to answer back. Rylie looked her helper over again and agreed with herself, she could see a social worker's closet filled with the type of clothing the woman was wearing, decent, but not expensive.

"I thought I was going to pee myself," Rylie said, changing the subject, finally on empty.

"Ready to get back into bed?" the woman asked.

"Yes please," Rylie said, not sure if she were actually in more pain, or just more aware since she'd pinched off her IV line. She waited for the other woman to help her up. "Thank you," Rylie grunted as she was helped back onto the bed. "Thank you," Rylie repeated as the woman picked up Rylie's legs and then tucked her under the stiff hospital sheets.

"That's what I'm here for," the woman said in a self-amused voice as she tucked Rylie in. Rylie brought her hands close to her sides and held them there, hugging her thighs as she settled into the now cool sheets.

"You okay?" the woman asked, rubbing Rylie's shoulder gently. Rylie unconsciously shrunk away from the woman's touch. "Rylie, you don't have to be scared," the woman said.

"What?" Rylie asked, nor sure she'd heard the woman correctly.

"You are safe Rylie," the woman said, squeezing Rylie's shoulder gently, the gesture meant to be comforting.

The words stole the breath from Rylie's lungs. Little shocks and tingles raced over her skin as goosebumps rose all over flesh. They knew who she was. Rylie's heart skipped a beat and then raced as if to make up for it. It was an unpleasant sensation. Tears formed in Rylie's eyes, large salty drops that clung to her corneas, obscuring her vision. She'd been so close. Just eleven months until she'd be outside the system's reach. She balled her fists at her sides, her jaw flexing as the fear and anxiety turned to anger. At the system, and at herself for the tears streaming down her face every time she blinked. She wasn't supposed to cry.

"You have no idea," Rylie said, her voice thick and heavy with emotion. She'd fled the system for good reasons.

"You are surrounded by good people and there is a uniformed guard sitting just outside your door," the woman assured her, misunderstanding the source of Rylie's fear. Rylie tried to smile, to pretend the words were a comfort.

"Thank you," Rylie said, not meaning it. She was rescued from having to say anything else when a nurse wearing pink scrubs knocked on the door and came in without waiting for a reply. She emptied the commode and told Rylie there was no blood in her urine as if that should make her happy. The nurse's mildly friendly attitude changed when the IV started to beep and alarm. The infusion pump was set to give pain meds on a timed schedule, and finding it couldn't because of the clamped line, started to alarm. "I'll pull the IV out if you restart it," Rylie said, sniffling in the snot that was threatening to trickle from her nose.

"Excuse me?" the nurse said, putting her hands on her hips.

"If you give me more pain meds I'll rip out the IV," Rylie said flatly.

The nurse was about to take Rylie to task when the other woman held up her hand, telling the nurse to let it go. Rylie watched the interaction, wondering if maybe she had been wrong. Did a social worker have that kind of pull over a nurse? Could the woman she'd just peed in front of be a doctor, maybe a psychiatrist?

"Are you sure you aren't in any pain?" the nurse asked again as she used a computer on the wall to document whatever it was she was doing. As the nurse was on the computer the other woman's phone rang. Rylie watched her helper fall back to the window as she greeted whomever was on the other end of the call.

"No pain," Rylie lied, "just thirsty." The nurse finished on the computer and disappeared for a minute before bringing back a tan plastic pitcher full of ice water. The nurse made sure the call bell was hanging within reach on the bed rail and looked one more time at Rylie, her eyebrows raised in question. She didn't think turning off the pain meds was a good idea. Rylie shook her head no. She was answering the nurse, but her attention was focused on the conversation by the window.

"No, agreed, there is no way this is related, the press have it as a low-level story, just an accidental bus strike," the woman said, her back to Rylie as she paused, listening to whomever was on her cell. Someone on the other side talked for a minute longer and then the woman said, "Thank you," and hung up, beaming as if she'd just been paid a huge complement.

She continued to stand near the window, tapping on her phone for a moment as Rylie poured some water and drank it, looking at her helper over the rim of her plastic cup with newfound concern. There was no way the woman was a social worker or a doctor. It was confirmed as the woman turned away from the window and Rylie saw the bulge on the woman's right hip under her jacket. She was carrying a firearm.

Rylie sipped at the ice water, her mind organizing the bits and pieces she was sure of. The woman in front of her wasn't a street cop, they didn't wear pant suits. That meant there was a detective in her room. The cop turned and walked back to the bed, pulling a small notebook out of an interior pocket. If she'd done that from the start Rylie was sure she never would have looked at the woman as anything but a cop.

"Do you remember what happened yesterday?" the women asked.

Rylie nodded no, not wanting to have to vocalize the memories of Sam attacking her.

"Did you know him? Did you know the man who attacked you?"

"I think I need an attorney," Rylie said, putting the cup down, her eyes locking on the other woman's. It was one of the things she'd learned from the street. If you were being questioned, ask for an attorney. The cops aren't allowed to keep talking to you if you ask for an attorney.

"Let's take a pause for a moment," her helper said, moving up to the side of the bed so she was right next to Rylie. "My name is Detective Parker and you aren't suspected of any wrong doing, okay Rylie?"

Detective Parker pulled a business card from her jacket and handed it to Rylie.

Rylie took the card and shook her head in the affirmative.

"I'm not trying to trick you," Parker said softly. "We have several witnesses that already told us you were attacked. I know you didn't do anything wrong, I'm just trying to see if you know why he was after you?"

Rylie took a deep breath before speaking. "I don't know why he was after me. I was just trying to get back to where I sleep at night."

"Did you know him?" Parker asked again.

Rylie swallowed, not sure if she was making a mistake by opening her mouth. "Not really. I'd seen him around, he was an alcoholic. I've seen him drinking with some other bums a few times. We all kind of recognize each other after a while," Rylie mumbled, ashamed that it was true. Parker stood there, waiting for her to continue. It made Rylie anxious. "He offered me booze a few times. I thought he just had a crush or something," Rylie said with disgust. "I just wanted to be left alone," Rylie said, unable to keep the tears from filling her eyes and rolling down her cheeks again. All she'd wanted was a hot dog. Rylie wiped her eyes with her hands and then quickly stuck them back under the covers, cursing herself. Detective Parker had never re-cuffed her, and Rylie wanted to keep it that way.

"Why are you here?" Rylie spit out quickly, watching as Parker's eyes scanned her, following the contour of her arms under the sheet.

"You came into the emergency department unconscious and badly contused from the scene of an assault," Parker said matter-of-factly.

"You don't put a cop on a runaway's door because they ran from social services," Rylie replied slowly, speaking the thought even as it formed.

"You're a smart kid, so why is there a guard on your door?" Parker asked, her expression changing slightly to something that might have been subdued amusement.

"First, I'm not a kid," Rylie said tersely. She didn't continue until Parker gave in and nodded agreement. "You're here because something weird happened last night between two homeless people, and you wanted to see if it was connected to the Red Summer killings." Rylie knew she had Parker by the way the cop's facial expression flickered with surprise before going carefully neutral.

"I guess I'm not the only one who's a detective here," Parker said, all traces of friendliness gone.

"So did the old guy have anything to do with what was going on?" Rylie asked.

Parker shook her head and breathed out wearily. "No, this was unrelated. I'm waiting on the tox screen but I'm guessing he got a bad batch of whatever he was into."

"Did he say why he attacked me?" Rylie asked. Parker paused, her eyebrows furrowing as she looked at Rylie. "Oh," Rylie said, her mouth a circle as she realized she'd asked a silly question. "The bus," Rylie said numbly, the sound of the tires and the hiss of the pneumatic breaks replaying in her memory.

"You were lucky," Parker said, trying to be positive.

"Why is your boss worried about the press then? It's just the start of a bad joke right?" Rylie asked, watching the detective closely. Rylie was doing her best to keep Parker off center, to make her forget that she'd never put her wrist back into the handcuffs.

"Bad joke?" Parker asked, one eyebrow rising.

"It sounds like the start of a bad joke to me," Rylie said. "A bus driver, a drunk hobo, and a homeless girl meet on the street," she said, letting the sentence trail off. Now that she thought about it, the punch line wasn't so good. "So your boss is worried about the tourism dollars?" Rylie asked, taking a more direct approach. She needed to keep Parker reacting instead of acting.

Parker stared at Rylie with a carefully neutral expression plastered on her face as she decided how to respond. "He has a duty to protect the people as well as the city. Since this isn't related, it doesn't make sense to stir up a lot of fear," Parker said defensively.

"But you just said this has nothing to do with the Red Summer killings. So what is your boss worried about?" Rylie pushed, watching Parker's face carefully as she spoke. At the mention of her boss Parker's brow pinched ever so slightly.

Rylie had found a crack in Detective Parker's armor.

"You don't need to worry about any of this," Parker said, emphasizing the word *any*.

"Oh, I think I understand," Rylie said. Parker settled back on her feet, her arms crossing in front of her as she stared at Rylie, all semblance of friendliness gone. "We were really close to the convention center, and your boss doesn't want any bad press while there is a huge conference in town."

"Don't make his motivations sound so horrible," Parker said icily.

"Wow, you're a mess," Rylie said with a laugh. "I wonder what the press would do with an anonymous tip about a possible Red Summer incident potentially being covered up by the police?" Rylie prodded.

"I didn't come here to spar with an angry teenager," Parker said, her voice hard.

Rylie didn't let the smile she was feeling touch her face. She was winning, now it was time to close the deal. "Is he married?" Rylie pushed. Parker froze, her lips becoming a thin line as she shoved the notebook back into her jacket pocket with exaggerated force. It was all Rylie needed to know she'd scored a hit, and possibly the win as Parker turned on her heel and walked to the door.

Rylie smiled at Parker's back. She'd won the match, and as long as things went well she'd be back out on the streets before morning, her aching ribs be damned. The thrill lasted until Parker touched the door handle, paused, and released it.

Parker turned slowly, her eyebrows furrowed in disbelief as

she walked back to Rylie's bedside. Rylie watched her cautiously. There was a subtle change in the way Parker moved. The confident energy the woman exuded now had an edge to it. Rylie wondered if she was about to regret pushing Parker too far.

"He is not married, and neither am I," Parker said pointedly, spitting out the words between a storm of raging emotions. Parker's face flushed with color and she looked away, not wanting to meet Rylie's eyes. Rylie cursed herself. She hadn't wanted to hurt Parker, she'd just wanted to throw the detective off balance enough so the other woman would forget to re-cuff her.

"I'm sorry," Rylie said truthfully. "I didn't mean to screw with your head."

"Is it so obvious?" Parker asked, her eyes looking anywhere but at Rylie.

"Not really, I think I'm just more tuned into what people are doing and saying. It helps me survive," Rylie said honestly. "I really didn't mean to make you feel bad. It's been a rough day for me too. I'm not quite myself."

Parker flexed her fingers around the guardrail of the bed, looking at Rylie, searching her face. Parker had that feeling she got when she was working a case and the bits of evidence were all there, she just wasn't connecting the pieces. Very slowly a smile turned up the corners of her lips and then spread across her face as she looked at the younger woman. "You are devious, aren't you?" she asked, her hand reaching out for the empty cuff to pull it from under the sheet. Rylie looked away as Parker held the cuff up, then shut her eyes and settled back into the pillow. She was beaten. She held her right hand out, her fingers shaking, offering her wrist to Parker.

"I really didn't mean to hurt you," Rylie said again, wincing as the cold metal touched her skin. Each metallic click of the cuff being tightened sounded like a hammer blow in her ears as Parker snugged the steel circle around her flesh.

"It's not too tight is it?" Parker asked, setting her hand on Rylie's forearm.

"More than you will ever know," Rylie said softly, not caring if Parker heard her or not. Rylie felt like screaming. How was she going to escape if she were handcuffed to a hospital bed? Parker squeezed Rylie's upper arm until the younger woman opened her eyes and looked up at her. Rylie expected to see something like smug victory on Parker's face, but the police detective wasn't gloating, Parker was looking at Rylie with the same expression she'd started with. It was something Rylie wasn't used to seeing.

Parker's face held nothing but genuine concern.

Rylie struggled with the mix of emotions flooding through her. Anger and fear raged, competing with a sense of guilt. How could Parker look at her with genuine concern after the way she'd just treated her? Rylie wasn't used to seeing concern when cops were looking at her. "I'm sorry if I touched a nerve, it wasn't about you. If you'd just left I would have been right behind you," Rylie mumbled, shameful heat rising in her neck.

"Is social services so bad?" Parker asked, her words gentle. She could see how much pain Rylie was in.

"You could leave me the key. I would say I stole it if they caught me again," Rylie said sadly, searching Parker's face, begging the detective to give her that one small thing.

"The doc said you are going to be sore for a few days but nothing was broken. They are going to discharge you tomorrow," Parker said cautiously. She spoke the next sentence very softly, as if she expected Rylie to rage at her. "Tomorrow you'll be discharged and social services will take you out to Ten Acres." Rylie shut her eyes, clamping them closed. It wasn't enough to keep the tears from escaping.

"Have you ever been to Ten Acres?" Rylie asked, her voice thick with emotions she couldn't control.

"Rylie, I know that Ten Acres will never be a real home, but at least it has warm food and you can sleep in a bed," Detective Parker said, her eyes searching Rylie's face.

"Do you realize two thirds of the staff at Ten Acres are males and that when they are short staffed they even let them monitor the female dorms at night?" The detective's eyebrows rose, her head moving slowly from side to side as she acknowledged Rylie's words.

"Is that why you stabbed a counselor in the neck with a pencil?" Parker asked.

"I don't know what you're talking about," Rylie said, refusing to admit what she'd done in case there was an assault charge coming her way.

"His version is that you stabbed him while making your escape," Parker informed her.

"I'm sure that's how it went down then," Rylie said bitterly. What was the point of arguing?

Parker looked at Rylie for a long time before she spoke. "It's going to be okay," she said, her voice increasing in volume as if saying it louder would make it true.

"Sure," Rylie, agreed half-heartedly.

"I've got to go make some calls and file some paperwork," Parker said, her face pained, her voice full of regret.

"And you get to just walk away," Rylie said resentfully beneath her breath as the detective walked out of her room.

Rylie used a corner of the covers to wipe the tears from her eyes and then her nose. She could see a small box of tissues on the nightstand two feet beyond her reach, she just wasn't willing to press the call bell and let the nurse and maybe the uniformed cop outside the door see her crying.

She lay in bed, angry that Sam had picked her to mess with, angry that they had identified her, and angry that Parker had realized she'd forgotten to cuff her again. The anger slowly turned to sullenness, then to boredom.

She was alone, handcuffed to her bed. The remote to the television hung on the bedrail, within reach of her free hand. She felt guilty turning the television on, as if it was a sign of weakness, of giving in. She flicked through the channels, trying to find something to distract her. The aches and pains the meds had been masking slowly grew in strength until she was glad to see the nurse who came to check on her.

Rylie didn't argue when the nurse offered her two pain pills, or care that the nurse had a smug look on her face as she washed the pills down with a sip of water. Rylie lay back, the television droning as the pain medicines dissolved in her belly and she fell into a deep sleep.

Chapter 6

Rylie felt horrible when she woke up.

She felt like all the moisture had been sucked out of her mucus membranes. Even her eyes were dry and scratchy. On top of that, everything hurt. She opened her eyes, looked at the beaming sun spilling through the window, and pinched them closed again. Part of her had hoped it was still the middle of the night, that she still had some time left before they took her to Ten Acres. She lay there, hoping the nurse would come in with more pain meds. For some reason, the thought of taking the meds by mouth was more acceptable than having them going directly into her veins.

She idly checked her right wrist. She was still handcuffed to the bed. She lay there, the anxiety slowly building. Every footstep she heard in the hallway sounded like a social worker coming to escort her away. How long had it been since she'd escaped? Almost three years? The same staff couldn't still be there, could they? Maybe it wouldn't be so bad now that she was older. She was so consumed with her thoughts she almost missed the soft sound of her door opening. She froze, staying very still, slowly becoming aware of the smell of coffee drifting on the air.

Rylie opened her eyes to slits, trying to see who was in her room without letting them know she was awake. Rylie froze when a shadow crossed between her and the window and a warm hand landed on her wrist, turning it so they could get to the handcuff lock. To Rylie it felt like being kicked in the groin. They weren't wasting any time dragging her out the hospital.

"I know you're awake," Parker said as she took the cuff off.

Rylie opened her eyes as she faked a yawn, pretending weakly to be waking up. She was surprised to see Parker standing next to her in street clothes. The detective was wearing a white blouse tucked into form fitting jeans. There was no gun in sight. "Sorry about the fit," the detective said, laying down a small stack of clothing on the end of the bed. "You're a bit thinner than me, but the jeans should be okay with the belt I brought. Get a shower and get dressed," she commanded as she walked out of the room. Rylie was too stunned to say anything. She hadn't expected to ever see Parker again. Shouldn't a social worker have come for her? Had the trick with the cuffs worried Parker so much she was going to hand her off to the Ten Acres staff herself?

Rylie growled at herself, refusing to let the aches and pains keep her in bed. She stood slowly, letting her sense of balance return before making her way into the bathroom. The pain in her ribs was a dull constant, reminding her she'd taken a beating. Even with the pain, it did feel good to be on her feet, under her own power.

She closed the bathroom door and stood in front of the mirror, shrugging off her gown. She winced as she examined herself. Her head was wrapped in gauze and her ribs were a patchwork of black and blue that stretched from her armpits down to her hips.

She unwound the gauze until she reached the final layer which was stuck to the back of her head with dried blood. It came free with a little pain and a few curse words. She tossed the bandage in the trash and took a long look at herself in the mirror, amazed at how quickly her fate had changed. She felt hopeless. What could she do? It made her think of her mother. Her mother must have repeated the serenity prayer at least once a week to her. Rylie said the words under her breath, watching them form on her lips in the mirror, "God grant me the serenity to accept the things I cannot change, courage to change the things I can, and the wisdom to know the difference."

She was going to Ten Acres. There was nothing she could do about it. Facing the reality made it easier to grab the toiletry kit and start moving. She would go to Ten Acres, and then she'd bolt the first chance she got. She accepted the short-term reality because the only other option was curling up on the floor and crying, and she wasn't going to allow self-pity to control her.

Rylie turned the shower on and let it run to warm up as she looked through the pink hospital bucket of personal hygiene products. There was soap, shampoo, a safety razor, and a nail file. She used the file to clean up the edges of her nails and then scrubbed her fingers with a washcloth until there was no dirt left. By the time she was done the shower was billowing steam. She felt the water with her hand and turned the temperature down just a little before stepping in, letting the heat wash over her, ignoring the stinging pain from the top of her head and all the little scratches she didn't realize she had. The pain didn't matter, the hot running water was glorious. Next came the safety razor. She shaved her legs, her groin, and then finished with her armpits. She wasn't naturally very hairy, but she figured if she was cleaning house she might as well take care of everything. It never occurred to her that she was stalling for every moment she could get before having to leave the hospital.

She took her time with the soap. She scrubbed herself clean and then stood under the hot water, pretending the world outside the bathroom didn't exist. Her hands were pruning when she finally shut the water off. It was time to be strong. To put a brave face on. She already had a plan. If she went into Ten Acres screaming and kicking they'd put her in the high security wing and keep her there until she turned eighteen. Instead she'd go in peacefully, resigned to her fate. She'd tell them whatever they wanted to hear, then, the moment they relaxed, she'd bolt.

Rylie stepped out of the shower and grabbed a towel. They smelled funny and were just as stiff as the sheets on the bed. She dried off before realizing she'd left the clothes Parker had brought her out in the room. She held a towel to her chest with one arm as she darted as fast as she could into the room to grab the clothes. The door to the hallway remained mercifully closed.

She sorted through the clothing; thankful that Parker had brought her a pair of new underwear, still in the packaging. Rylie lived on the street, but wearing someone else's undies was gross. She slid the plain cotton underwear on and picked up the stretchy tank top bra. It still had a tag on it from the store. Rylie tore the tag off and slipped it on.

Rylie raked her fingers through her hair carefully, avoiding the wound on the back of her head as she looked at herself in the foggy mirror with a smile. She looked like she was about to do a bad music video or go to a yoga class. It made Rylie glad Parker had put a tee-shirt in the mix as well. Rylie liked layers. She finished dressing, cinching the belt tight to keep the jeans from falling off her.

She didn't notice the pair of running shoes on her tray

table until she came out of the bathroom. She picked up the shoes, then noticed the card that Parker had given her the day before was sitting nearby. She picked it up and smiled before slipping it into her back pocket. When Rylie went to pull the shoes on she discovered that Parker had thought of everything. A pair of socks has been stuffed into one of the shoes.

Rylie was sitting on the chair next to the hospital bed tying her shoes when someone knocked on the door. It opened just enough for Parker to speak through the crack. "You decent?" she asked.

"Yep," Rylie said, double knotting the shoelace.

"You clean up well," the detective said, scanning Rylie as she came in. "Sorry about the fit," she apologized as she saw how the jeans were cinched around Rylie's waist.

"Don't be, I really appreciate the clothes. It was a very nice thing to do," Rylie said, trying to look out into the hall behind the detective. She had a knot in her stomach. The corridor was full of normal hospital activity but she didn't see anyone waiting to take her to Ten Acres.

"You don't need to think about running," Parker said, following Rylie's gaze.

"Not going to run, I won't repay your kindness like that," Rylie said, smoothing her shirt over her stomach. She didn't feel like she was technically lying. By the time she ran Parker wouldn't even remember her. Rylie figured it would take at least a few weeks for the staff at Ten Acres to trust her enough to let down their guard.

"Is it really that bad?"

"You have different prisons for different types of criminals, right?" Rylie asked.

Parker nodded. "Generally speaking mixing your jay walkers with your killers is a bad idea."

"Well, Ten Acres is where they send the kids who have already failed at foster care, who failed at halfway houses. It's the violent kids, the rule breakers, and even the well intentioned staff get rough around the edges when they face that every day. Some of the kids have been there since they were ten or eleven. They are at the top of the food chain. If you keep your head down and follow the rules I guess you might be okay. I'm just not that much of a follower," Rylie admitted, smiling apologetically.

"You don't talk like a seventeen-year-old," Parker said thoughtfully.

"I'm almost eighteen," Rylie said defensively before they both turned to face each other and smiled. It was such a juvenile response to the question.

"You need anything else from here?" Parker asked, changing subjects.

"No," Rylie said, girding herself for what was to come, trying to see around the detective again.

"It's just me," Parker promised with a smile.

"You mean there isn't a social worker?"

"Not as long as you are okay with it? It is Saturday, and I'm technically not working, but I volunteered to help out a little this morning."

"Yes, I'm okay with it," Rylie said, trying to smile through the slowly growing anxiety. It was time to leave the hospital. It was time to go to Ten Acres. Rylie appreciated Parker giving her the clothes and trying to make the trip easier - it didn't change where she'd be sleeping at the end of the day though. The first night she'd spent at the facility last time had not been fun. There had been a bit of hazing, and she'd broken the rules by fighting back. It had only gotten worse from there.

Even so, walking out of the hospital and through the parking garage to Parker's car was oddly thrilling. Rylie had expected to feel like a prisoner being transported, but Parker just walked beside her, treating her like anyone else. It was not how Rylie had pictured things in her head. Parker even let her get in the front seat of her unmarked car.

"How do you feel about religion?" Parker asked after they'd driven a short while.

Rylie put her hand on her chin, thinking before she answered. "Not too big on god," she said honestly, looking at Parker cautiously, not sure where the conversation was going or if Parker was maybe a secret Jesus freak?

"Can you fake it?"

"What?"

"Can you fake it?" Parker asked again more pointedly.

"I can if I need to," Rylie said, feeling uneasy, wondering what Parker was working up to.

"Good, I spent some time on the phone last night and pulled a few strings to make sure you didn't end up back at Ten Acres," Parker said quickly, her hands locked on the wheel. "I was able to get you a bed at the school for girls at Saint Mary's. I had to call in some favors." Parker sounded nervous; as if she wasn't sure she'd done the right thing.

"You're kidding, right?" Rylie asked, turning in her seat to face Parker, too stunned to believe what she was hearing.

Parker glanced at her with a hard look, telling Rylie with her eyes that there are some things you don't kid about. "Oh, I think I'll look good in a plaid skirt," Rylie assured her with a smile. "Why didn't you tell me back in the hospital?" Rylie asked after they'd driven a little further.

"I needed to know if you would try and bolt the moment we walked out of the door," Parker said bluntly. "I'd rather know now if I can't trust you. If you burn me here I'm screwing a friend. I don't want that to happen," she said honestly.

"I'll be good, I promise," Rylie said, feeling suddenly light. She wasn't going back to Ten Acres!

"You eat meat right?" Parker asked, turning into the parking lot of a burger joint.

"Yep."

"And you're not going to try and run?" Parker said, her eyes shifting to that look parents got when they are trying to tell if you are lying.

"Not unless you let them put guacamole on my burger," Rylie promised.

"No guacamole," Parker said with a smile.

Rylie waited for Parker to get out and walk to the front of the car before she climbed out to join her. She wanted the detective to feel comfortable. The anxiety and sense of impending doom which had been hanging over her had evaporated, leaving her giddy with relief as they walked into the restaurant. Parker led her to the massive menu board near the counter. It listed out over a hundred different combinations of burgers. Rylie looked at the board and laughed, thinking it was a waste, the only thing a burger needed was cheese and bacon.

The burgers were huge, easily five inches across. Rylie ate the first few bites slowly, savoring the beef and the bacon. It had been a long time since she'd had a good burger. When she splurged on fast food quantity was more important than quality.

They ate in silence for a time. Parker waited until they were both stuffed, looking at the food still left on their trays, to continue the conversation. "You must have really made someone mad at Ten Acres," Parker said, wiping her mouth with a napkin.

"What do you mean?"

"When I called the social worker yesterday to let her know what was going on she told me she already had three calls from Ten Acres about your intake," Parker said.

"I really can't thank you enough," Rylie said, a touch of the dread from the morning pulling the color from her face.

"Well, hopefully no one there has any pull, I'll file your transport paperwork on Monday just to cover my ass though," Parker said, pulling some money out of her wallet to leave a tip.

"Your boss will cover for you with family services, won't he?" Rylie asked. She was hoping the detective and her boss were a thing now. He wouldn't leave her hanging if he was trying to get into Parker's pants.

"It's really not like that. There is a," Parker said, pausing, knowing exactly what Rylie had been thinking, "tension between us. But it can never happen. I work for him and it's the type of thing that destroys a squad. He doesn't want anyone thinking he's playing favorites."

"That sucks, so he is overcompensating and being harder on you than everyone else," Rylie said.

Parker laughed and shook her head. "If I didn't know your age I'd swear you were a weathered forty year old with ten kids."

"Ah, thanks - I guess," Rylie said with a smirk, knowing Parker had meant it as a complement. "But seriously, thank you for everything," she added, her voice nearly breaking as she said the words. She took a quick bite and hid behind the burger. Rylie was not used to letting her emotions show through.

Parker smiled.

It was turning out to be a beautiful day.

Chapter 7

Rylie looked up at the massive stone building, dwarfed by its size. The church was imposing, even awe inspiring, its front taking up a full city block. Parker slowed down as they cruised by the gothic stone facade, letting Rylie get the full effect of the towering spires and beautiful stained-glass windows, remembering the first time she'd stood in front of Saint Mary's herself. Rylie didn't see the heartfelt smile that touched Parker's lips as they drove by the building.

At the corner Parker turned and drove to the rear of the complex, pulling into a parking lot. Rylie found it slightly jarring how the scenery had changed. She could still see the top of the church's spires, but the parking lot was surrounded by a high fence and square, institutional buildings. Parker shut off the engine and looked at Rylie nervously.

Rylie smiled and give Parker two thumbs up. She had no intention of burning Parker, but she didn't waste the words, Rylie was smart enough to know the only way to convince Parker was by showing her. She'd be a model of discipline and self-control. Even if it were horrible – it couldn't be as bad as Ten Acres – and it was only until she turned eighteen. Rylie promised herself she'd do her time and move on.

"Please be nice to the sisters, they really do care," Parker said as she walked Rylie to a solid looking security door. A camera watched them from above the door as Parker raised her hand, about to put her thumb on the intercom call button.

"I promise to be good," Rylie said with a smile. Parker

sighed lightly and leaned into the button. She wanted this to work out and not just because she'd pulled in favors. She wanted Rylie to get off the streets. She wanted Rylie to be safe. The thought gave Parker pause. She had an intense desire to make sure Rylie was safe. Part of it was easy for her to understand, but she'd worked with other troubled teens before and not gotten so involved. The depths of her feelings surprised her.

There was a brief delay before they were buzzed in.

"Parker," it is so good to see you again," an older woman wearing a nun's tunic said as soon as the door was open enough for Rylie to see inside.

"Sister Kathy," Parker said warmly, giving the woman a solid hug before stepping back. "Thank you so much for your help," Parker, said, stressing the thank you before turning to introduce Rylie.

Rylie wasn't sure what she was supposed to do so she stuck her hand out to shake. The sister took her hand and gripped it firmly, "I'm Sister Kathy," she said with a smile.

"Rylie Sampson," Rylie said, taking in the sister. Sister Kathy's hair was almost completely gray but the hand that gripped hers was strong and the sisters eyes were sharp and intelligent.

"It is a pleasure to meet you," Sister Kathy said, her voice full of genuine warmth before leading them inside the building. They were in a short hallway with a few doors on one side. "Why don't you have a seat," Sister Kathy said, pointing to a well-worn bench along the wall, just outside a small office. Rylie sat down, her butt sliding on the polished wood as Parker and the nun went into the office. "I just have a few things for Detective Parker to sign and then we'll show you around and introduce you to everyone," Sister Kathy said warmly. Rylie watched as Parker and the nun disappeared into the office. Rylie wondered how many kids Parker had brought to Saint Mary's over the years. Sister Kathy and Parker were clearly friends.

"Okay," Rylie mumbled to the empty hallway, clasping her hands together in front of her so she didn't fidget. She was excited and scared, wondering what Saint Mary's had in store for her. The delicious burger she'd eaten was sitting heavily in her stomach though. She couldn't help but wonder what the next few months were going to be like. Rylie concentrated on breathing as she listened to Parker and Sister Kathy's muted chatting in the office. She could hear them, but not really make out what they were saying. It struck her how ordinary the day seemed for them. They even laughed now and then. It felt so strange to Rylie, she was having a major life changing event while Parker and Sister Kathy were having what seemed like a normal day.

Rylie bolted upright when the door to the office finally opened. "Sister Kathy is going to show you around," Parker said, looking at Rylie with a raised eyebrow. Rylie shrugged nervously, not sure what the proper response was. Parker put a hand on Rylie's shoulder and squeezed gently, trying to tell her it was going to be okay. Rylie grabbed her quickly, hugging Parker and then letting her go equally as fast, her face coloring in embarrassment. It surprised Rylie just as much as it did Parker. "It's going to be okay," Parker promised, smiling encouragingly.

"We'll take good care of you," Sister Kathy promised,

taking Rylie's elbow and pulling her away from Parker. Sister Kathy lead Rylie down the hallway as Parker stood unmoving, watching as Rylie disappeared into the depths of Saint Mary's.

"We consider everyone here at Saint Mary's a family," Sister Kathy said as they walked. "Every new student gets a big sister to show her around and help her. Donna is going to be your big, she will make sure you don't get lost and help you learn the rules." It sounded like a speech Sister Kathy had given many times.

The Sister kept talking as she led Rylie into the dorms. Rylie nodded her head at the appropriate times but she was overwhelmed, hearing but not storing half of what the Sister was saying. The shock of not being taken to Ten Acres still filled her with excitement and a sense of relief. It made it hard to concentrate. The dorms were a series of identical square rooms spaced out on either side of a hallway. Each room held a set of bunk beds against the walls and four heavy duty wardrobes. Rylie couldn't help but notice the smaller, institutional details though. Everything was bolted down, and the windows in the dorms were small and set high up on the walls, close to the ceiling. Sister Kathy showed Rylie to her new bed before opening the wardrobe next to it. "You can put your things in here," the Sister said.

"All I have is what I'm wearing," Rylie said, suddenly embarrassed.

"No shame in that girl," Sister Kathy said. "Sister Ida runs the donation center, I'll have her get you some clothes tonight."

"Thank you," Rylie mumbled, nervous and self-conscious as she looked around the room. All the bunks were made, some more neatly than others, and while the room was clean, it also showed the evidence of being lived in. Rylie looked at her bunk, wondering if the Sister would let her lie down and hide under the covers. As much as she wanted to avoid it, she knew she couldn't. She was going to come face to face with a group of teenage girls very soon.

"It's okay to be nervous, it will feel more like home in a few days," Sister Kathy assured Rylie, guiding her back out into the hallway.

Rylie looked around as the Sister led the way, trying to keep her fingers still. When she was anxious she tended to fidget. The hallways and rooms they passed were empty. The place was too quiet. Rylie laced her fingers together on her belly and slowly increased the pressure until her knuckles were turning white. How could the absence of others, and the knowledge she was about to meet a bunch of new people, both equally set her on edge? She was trying to figure it out when the Sister opened a door and revealed a room full of teenage girls. As the door opened the sound of multiple voices, laughter, and general mayhem slipped out. It fell to a low murmur as the Sister held the door open and Rylie stepped in.

The large room was dominated by several folding tables which had been arranged down its center. One side of each table was stacked with supplies. Girls lined the other, each of them frozen, all eyes on the new girl. Sister Kathy cleared her throat as she followed Rylie in, letting the door shut behind her with a bang. The sound startled everyone back into motion.

The first two girls in the line were taking flattened boxes and opening them. They put two bands of tape across the bottoms before passing the boxes down the line. At the next station four cans of soup were put in before continuing its journey down the length of the table. Each person put something in the box until the last girl taped it shut and two other girls picked them up from the end of the table and stacked them on a half-filled pallet. An ancient Nun watched over the activities, a pair of small circular glasses perched on her nose. All the girls were wearing the same dark blue tee shirt with white block lettering on them saying FOOD DRIVE.

"Girls," Sister Kathy said, her voice filling the room, "this is Rylie Sampson."

"Hello, Rylie," nineteen voices replied, their hands continuing to work even as all their eyes locked on the newcomer. Rylie waved back weakly, fighting the urge to run and hide. She did not like being the center of attention. Rylie knew her Big Sister the moment she saw her. The girl pointed at herself, then Rylie, then back at herself, a huge grin on her face. Rylie waved again, trying to give her new Big Sister a genuine smile in return.

"Donna will show you around from here," Sister Kathy said, patting Rylie on her shoulder before leaving. Rylie flinched as the door behind her shut heavily, standing there feeling as if everyone's eyes were looking at her.

Donna came to Rylie's rescue, or at least tried to. She walked up to Rylie and made a halting attempt to hug her before pulling away with a pained cringe when Rylie tensed at the attempted contact. "Sorry, I have to work on not being so touchy," Donna said quickly without taking a breath, her eyes locked on Rylie's.

Rylie stood still, taking in the other girl. Donna was about her height but any similarity ended there. Donna was pale, the kind of pale you normally associate with red heads who are so easily burned in the sun that they don't go outside without aluminum foil grade suntan lotion on, while Rylie was on the opposite end of the skin tone spectrum. Where Rylie's face was long and narrow with hair that fell to her shoulders, Donna had a round face and wore her hair so short it stood straight up without any help from mousse or hairspray. They were as different at first glance as two people could be – and yet Rylie looked at the openness, the happiness, on the other girl's face and immediately liked her.

"It's okay," Rylie assured her new friend with a smile, barely tensing when Donna took her upper arm and guided her back to the table.

"Everyone here is really nice," Donna said, pulling Rylie to her station.

Rylie picked up toothbrushes and handed them to Donna in pairs as the other girl grabbed travel size tubes of toothpaste and stuck everything in the closest box before pushing it down to the next station. Donna talked nonstop, pausing only long enough to breath or look over at Rylie to get a nod or grunt of agreement before continuing. Rylie smiled and nodded as Donna told her about her favorite girl bands and television shows. Rylie noted that a lot of the shows that Donna liked seemed to be kids programming. Rylie smiled and laughed with Donna when she said something intentionally goofy, and struggled for several minutes when trying to decide if her Big was just a really sweet kid or maybe a bit delayed. In the end,

Rylie figured it was likely a combination of both.

It was something else about Donna the perfect Big Sister though. She was so honest, so full of lightness that it was nearly impossible to get irritated with her. She was overflowing with a sweetness that was coupled with an innate sense for what others were feeling. Within ten minutes of sitting next to Rylie, Donna apologized again for the attempted hug, telling Rylie it was okay if she didn't like to be touched. The fact that Donna picked up on it, and then tried to be comforting about it, made Rylie feel bad for wondering if her Big was a little delayed a few minutes before. Donna might come off as a few years younger than her physical age but she was also naturally intuitive and in touch with what was going on around her.

When two pallets of hurricane relief were loaded with boxes, it was free time. Several of the girls stopped and gave quiet words of welcome to Rylie before they disappeared into the hallway.

"Are you ready for the grand tour?" Donna asked, holding open the door for Rylie.

"Sure," Rylie said, figuring a little refresher wouldn't hurt. Donna walked her back to the dorms, which Rylie had already seen, then took her to the gymnasium which could have been pulled out of either of the two public schools Rylie had attended as a child. Donna pointed to the rolled down aluminum shutters at one end of the gym and explained the gymnasium also doubled as their dining hall. There was also a large locker room, which Rylie was glad to see had separate shower stalls with heavy vinyl curtains, and a laundry room with four washers and four dryers. They found most of the other girls in the TV room where one wall of the room was dominated by a massive, boxy television. Two sectional couches cut the TV room in half. The area behind the couches was occupied by a scuffed-up ping pong table.

Sister Ida intercepted Rylie and Donna as they were leaving the TV room and handed her an armful of clothing and towels. The sister followed them back to the dorms, asking Rylie a series of questions that started with her shoe size and ended with her cup size. The two smallest bras she had were going to be too big. Sister Ida seemed put off by the fact she didn't have everything Rylie needed.

"It's okay, I don't really need a bra," Rylie said, trying to be nice. There were some advantages to having small boobs.

It was the wrong thing to say.

"It's not right for a girl to walk around without a brazier," Sister Ida said sternly, before promising to get Rylie a bra the next day, even if she had to go out and buy one. Rylie tried to show Sister Ida the sports bra Parker had given her, but the Sister appeared to think it was just a tight tee shirt.

The Sister stalked off, shaking her head in disgust.

Donna waited until the Sister was gone before busting out in laughter. "Be careful when you are doing your laundry or that sports bra is going to go missing," she warned.

"Speaking from experience?" Rylie asked.

"Not me, but one of the other girls found a pair of short shorts in the clothing donations and they disappeared within a week. None of us know for sure, but Sister Ida is on the top of the suspect list for sure," Donna said with a smile.

"I'll have to remember that," Rylie said as she packed her

newfound clothing away in the wardrobe next to her bunk. "I have to pee and want to try these on as pajamas," Rylie said, holding up the sweat pants Sister Ida had built her stack of donated clothes on.

"That's the only bad part," Donna said, leading Rylie out of their dormitory.

"Bad part?" Rylie asked curiously.

"The closest bathrooms are in the locker rooms off the gym and it's a long walk when you're half asleep," Donna complained. "I try not to drink anything after dinner."

"Ah," Rylie said, nodding her head in mock understanding. She was willing to bet it was still better than peeing while leaning against a concrete wall, hoping no one came around the corner. Sometimes you had to go and there wasn't a fast food joint nearby. Donna stood outside the stall as Rylie peed and switched her pants, chatting the whole time. "These are so comfy," Rylie said, coming out in a baggy pair of sweat pants.

On their way out of the bathroom Donna slipped her arm through Rylie's so they were bound together at the elbow. Rylie wanted to pull away but was afraid she'd hurt Donna's feelings. They were halfway back to the TV room when Donna stopped and pulled her arm away with an angry look on her face. "I'm really sorry," Donna said, accenting her words with an angry little stomp of a foot. Rylie raised an eyebrow, not sure what was going on. "I'm trying not to hang on you," Donna blurted out, "but then I forgot. I'm just a really touchy feely person."

Rylie could see the tears welling in Donna's eyes. Her Big was being absolutely serious. It made Rylie feel extra bad for having to clamp down her own reactions and not laugh. It wasn't a mean laugh, more of the absurd kind, but Rylie knew that Donna would never understand that. "It's okay Donna," Rylie said, speaking slowly, turning the other girl so they were standing face to face.

Donna nodded, wiping tears away from her eyes before they could fall. "You're sure?"

"Yep, no worries," Rylie promised, holding out the crook of her elbow for Donna to take again. It wasn't necessarily the first thing that Rylie wanted to do, but letting Donna suffer felt wrong, like kicking a puppy. Donna put her arm back through Rylie's with a smile and hugged it.

"I'm glad you are here," Donna said, a new spring in her step as they continued down the hall.

"Me too," Rylie said, and meant it. She was glad she was there and even more happy that Donna was. Donna wouldn't have lasted a day at Ten Acres.

The other girls at Saint Mary's were nice enough. They left Rylie alone but didn't exclude her at the same time. They waved or said a quiet hello when Rylie and Donna returned to the TV room before turning back to their show. Rylie was more than fine with it, she didn't like too much attention. Donna found them a section of couch and then grabbed a bag of popcorn from one of the other girls. The two new friends watched TV and ate popcorn. Rylie had no idea who any of the characters were, but the show was silly and not hard to follow. She found herself laughing with everyone else, her voice mingling with the groups. It would have been a perfect evening but for one little uncomfortable moment when the volume dipped and the whole room heard one of the girls on the far end of the couch complaining that they were all on lockdown again. Donna hissed at the girl in a surprising display of anger and patted Rylie's hand. Rylie wasn't even upset, she was more touched that Donna was sticking up for her.

"Don't worry about them, the Sisters just don't want you to feel left out if you were the only one not allowed to leave the school. Not the smartest way to make everyone else like you, but the Sisters mean well," Donna said into Rylie's ear.

A bell rang when it was time for dinner and all the girls headed for the gymnasium. After they ate Rylie and Donna played ping pong and watched more TV until another bell rang and it was time to head back to the dorms and get ready for bed.

Rylie climbed into her assigned bunk and pulled the covers up to her chin, prepared for a long night. She thought she would have a difficult time falling asleep with strangers all around her, but the bed was soft, and the air conditioning was just low enough to make the light blanket she pulled up to her neck a necessity. She fell asleep easily and slept through the night.

Donna woke Rylie up early the next morning. It was Sunday and she wanted to eat breakfast before they went to mass. Rylie rolled out of bed slowly, grunting in pain as her body reminded her just how bruised it still was. "You okay?" Donna asked, looking at Rylie with a raised eyebrow.

"I'll be good once I start moving," Rylie said, forcing herself to smile at Donna. She held in the curses she wanted to say as she changed back into the jeans Parker had given her, afraid Donna would make her visit the school nurse if the girl knew how sore she was.

Donna chatted while they walked towards the gym for breakfast, oblivious to how stiffly Rylie was walking. They lined up behind other girls, grabbed metal trays and shuffled by the serving window that separated the gym from the kitchen. It reminded Rylie of distant memories of grade school. As each girl took their breakfast they thanked the portly older woman serving them. Rylie followed their lead.

After eating breakfast and sitting through a forty-minute mass Sister Kathy informed the girls that they had a half hour before they should meet by the rear exit.

"Where are we going?" Rylie asked Donna as they walked to the bathrooms and stood in front of two sinks to wash their faces.

"Well, some of the girls are going to help out at the soup kitchen but we could stay here and watch TV if you wanted," Donna said, watching Rylie in the mirror as she spoke, her eyes narrowing as she measured Rylie's response.

"Do you think they will let me go? I don't plan on running. I like it here," Rylie said, staring back at Donna's reflection until the other girl nodded.

"I think they will," Donna said, continuing to nod her head.

They made a quick stop in the dorms for Donna to change shirts before heading to the rear entrance. When they got there, they found the other girls lined up against the wall, ready to go. Sister Kathy walked down the line, greeting each girl with a friendly word. When Sister Kathy reached Donna and Rylie she stopped and chatted a little longer. "How was your first night?" Sister Kathy asked.

"I slept like a baby, and Donna has been the best Big I could have hoped for," Rylie said honestly. Sister Kathy seemed pleased, nodding her head before returning to the front of the line. Rylie never saw the little thumbs up that Donna gave the sister.

Rylie was glad the bus was heading into downtown, away from her normal haunts. Seeing other men and women she'd bummed around with would have been awkward. When they got to the food kitchen Rylie tried to ignore the fact that Sister Ida always seemed to be right behind her when she turned around and that Donna never left her side. Rylie concentrated on serving soup, happy to be helping. It hit her as she was helping others that she had no intention of running from Saint Mary's, and not just because of her promise to Parker. The place felt good. It was not something Rylie was used to feeling.

After washing dishes everyone piled back into the bus and returned to Saint Mary's. The girls got off the bus and huddled near the rear entrance, everyone looking at Sister Kathy. Rylie picked up on the energy and poked Donna in the side to get her attention. Donna spoke into Rylie's ear, "Oh, Sunday afternoon is supposed to be leisure time. I think everyone is trying to figure out what the Sisters are going to do since they let you go to the soup kitchen."

"I really don't want to ruin everyone's plans," Rylie said quietly.

"I think I can fix it," Donna said softly before raising her voice. "Sister Kathy," Donna said, then repeated it more loudly until all eyes were on her.

"Yes, Donna?" Sister Kathy asked.

"Would it be okay if Rylie and I stayed in and cleaned the Church today?" The other girls reacted with excitement, they thought it was a great idea. Sister Kathy held up a finger to get everyone to quiet down. The Sister looked at Rylie, who smiled and gave her a thumbs up – and it was decided.

After Sister Kathy released the girls to use their free time however they wanted several of them ran up to Donna and gave her quick hugs before scattering. Rylie mouthed, "thank you," to her Big and was happy to see Donna glowing. Donna found a simple solution that left everyone happy – and if that meant Rylie had to clean a church, she was just fine with that.

"It usually only lasts a month or two," Donna said as they walked into the school. "You know, if you behave," she added, looking at Rylie with a touch of hesitation.

"Why wouldn't I behave?" Rylie asked. Rylie had meant it lightheartedly but Donna bit her lip and looked around helplessly as if she'd been yelled at. "Spit it out," Rylie said, poking Donna's arm, encouraging her to speak.

"We were told not to ask you about your past unless you brought it up, but Margaret said she heard you were homeless and tried to kill yourself by throwing yourself in front of a bus."

Rylie laughed and shook her head. "I was homeless, but I never tried to kill myself. There was a," Rylie paused, trying to figure out how to word what happened to cause the least amount of follow up questions, "disturbance on the sidewalk. I ended up in the street and got hit by a bus."

"Holy crap, you really were hit by a bus," Donna said, astounded. She asked Rylie ten different ways as they walked to the church what it felt like? What did Rylie remember? Had she peed herself? Rylie answered the questions as best she could and tried not to laugh when Donna asked if Rylie had checked her fillings when she woke up in the hospital. Donna was under the impression that people in car accidents routinely had their fillings pop out. Rylie wondered if the source of the information had been a cartoon but kept her mouth shut.

Getting into the church from the school meant finding Sister Ida to let them in, then taking a long walk. They passed the dorms, the gym, and the locker rooms before finally coming to a large non-descript steel door at the end of a hallway. Sister Ida produced a key ring with a total of three keys on it and proceeded to try all three before successfully unlocking the door with the last key. The door opened into a storage room filled with religious ornaments and candelabra and holiday decorations. Sister Ida led the way through the storage room to another door which opened into the church's main entry. The smell of old wood and lemon scented polish filled the air the moment the Sister opened the door.

Rylie stopped at the entry into the church and stared as Donna retrieved a cleaning cart from a nearby closet. Donna pulled the cart up next to Rylie and stopped, taking in the cavernous space. Donna had walked into the church a hundred times, but it was still impressive. She stood next to Rylie, giving her friend time to take it in. The ceiling soared above them, supported by massive wooden arches carved with angels ascending into the heavens. At the far end of the church the pipes of an organ rose three stories up the wall, a magnificent back drop behind the pulpit.

"I'll be in the balcony reading if you need me," Sister Ida said, turning to leave them to their work. Donna and Rylie turned to watch the Sister disappear up a wide set of stairs off to the left.

"She'll be snoring in about fifteen minutes," Donna shared

with a wink.

Donna pushed the cart to the front of the church and handed Rylie a dusting rag and a can of spray polish. Donna worked the back rests of the pews while Rylie did the seats. They polished for a little while in silence before Donna asked, "How long were you on the street?"

"A few years," Rylie said, trying to keep it vague.

"That's a long time," Donna said, shivering at the thought.

"How long have you been at Saint Mary's?" Rylie asked, hoping to change the subject from her own life.

"Since I was twelve. I turn eighteen next year," Donna said, her face pinching up as she said it. Donna didn't want to think about being a legal adult. Once she graduated from high school she wouldn't be able to stay at Saint Mary's. Rylie could see the anxiety in Donna's face. Her Big was very easy to read.

"Were you on the streets before?" Rylie asked carefully, not sure if it was an off-limits topic. "If it's okay to ask?" she added quickly.

Donna paused, leaning back into the pew she'd just polished. "I haven't talked about this in a long time," she said, running a hand through her short hair absent mindedly.

"You don't have to if you don't want to," Rylie said softly, sliding across the wooden pew until she was sitting next to Donna, the sides of their legs touching.

"You know why I cut my hair so short?" Donna asked. Rylie shook her head. She had no idea. "My mother's boyfriend liked to hit her. When I was eleven I came home one day and he was really working her over. When she couldn't fight anymore he turned on me. He held me down by my hair, pinning my head to the floor," she said, choking up. Donna's eyes glazed over as she remembered, her mouth opening to speak but just hanging open.

Rylie's heart sank, she could see the pain wash over Donna. She carefully took Donna's hand in hers and squeezed it, willing her Big strength. Donna shook her head, breaking free of the memory enough to speak as tears ran down her cheeks. "He raped me. I tried to keep my eyes closed. Every time I opened them I was looking at my mother's body in the kitchen. I wanted to turn away, but he had my hair pulled so tight I could barely move." Donna sniffled, trying to pretend the tears weren't running freely down her face. It made Donna feel guilty because Sister Kathy kept telling her she needed to be tougher.

"I'm so sorry," Rylie said, grabbing Donna and pulling her into a fierce hug. Rylie had lost her mother to cancer, she knew the pain of loss. She couldn't imagine it being compounded by violence and rape.

Donna continued to speak, tears soaking into Rylie's tee-shirt. "When he was done, he sat in his lounge chair and drank until he passed out. I went into my room and cut off all my hair." Donna paused, relaxing into Rylie's hug. It felt nice to be held. "I left the apartment and tried to live on the streets. I'm not sure how long I lasted. I got picked up by a cop for stealing food at the supermarket. I was someplace scary for a few nights, then I went to court, and ever since then, I've been at Saint Mary's."

"It's okay, let it out," Rylie encouraged. She could feel Donna's heart racing against her.

It was a long while before Donna lifted her head and wiped her tears away. "I really do like this place," she said. "I don't want to graduate," she added.

"They aren't going to kick you out onto the street. Sister Kathy has to have a plan," Rylie said, hoping, praying she wasn't talking out her ass.

"That's what Sister Kathy says. She says I already have a bed at a halfway house where they will train me for *life skills*," she made air quotes with her fingers as she said it. "I wish I could stay here forever though," she said, standing back up and spraying the back of the pew, going back to work. "I love the smell of the church," she said. A moment later she giggled and stopped, tilting her head as she listened. She pointed above them, her head tilted. Rylie tilted her own head and smiled as she realized she could hear Sister Ida's snoring coming from above them.

They worked in silence for a while before Donna spoke again, her words hesitant. "I still thought of myself as a virgin," Donna said quietly, not looking at Rylie as she worked.

"You were, that is something for you to give," Rylie said, trying to sound confident in her answer. Rylie had never even let a boy feel her up so she wasn't an expert when it came to sex - but she knew what Donna was getting at. Donna didn't care about the technical definition of virginity; she was talking about the willing act.

"I lost my virginity on the altar boy cushions," Donna said as if she were asking for the salt at the dinner table.

"What?" Rylie blurted out, looking from Donna to the benches where the altar boys sat with shock on her face. Donna smiled and giggled when she saw the surprise on Rylie's face. "With an altar boy?" Rylie asked in disbelief.

"No," Donna said emphatically as if that would have made losing her virginity in a church a potentially sinful event. "His name was Aaron, the sisters paid him to mow the lawn, sweep the floors, and empty the trash cans. We used to clean the church together until he graduated from high school and joined the Marines."

"And the sisters?" Rylie asked incredulously.

"Sister Ida is a pretty sound sleeper," Donna said with a smile and a laugh.

"And you never got caught?" Rylie asked, nodding up to the balcony and the sounds of snoring.

"No, at least not that I know of," Donna said, thinking about it with a shrug.

Rylie didn't know what to say so she just nodded her head and kept cleaning.

"You don't think I'm a slut do you?" Donna asked when we reached the end of the row and moved to the next.

"Aaron made you happy?"

"He did, he was nice," Donna said.

"I think that's all that matters, isn't it?" Rylie asked.

"Hell yes," Donna said whole heartedly. Rylie wondered if truer words had been said in the church lately.

The two worked their way through the church, cleaning and talking. The longer they worked together the more Rylie wanted to thank Parker. Saint Mary's had rules and the sisters didn't trust her yet, but Rylie felt very lucky she'd ended up there. Spending just a few hours with Donna sparked something Rylie had repressed for a long time. It felt good to let her guard down and just spend time with another person. It felt good to have someone to talk to. Rylie was a little sad when they reached the last pew and it was time to go back to the dorms.

"There are two extra bonuses to staying in when everyone else goes out. You can watch whatever you want on the TV and you can take as long as you want in the shower," Donna said as they headed for their dorm and Sister Ida went to her office. When they reached the dorms, Donna grabbed clean clothes and a plastic carrier full of bathroom supplies as Rylie pulled out her sweats and her last clean pair of underwear. "Don't worry, you can use my stuff," Donna said, shaking her basket of soap, shampoo, and other bathroom supplies.

The combination bathroom and locker room was old but clean. Pale tile covered every surface. Donna went to the sinks and set down her toiletries. "You mind giving me a hand?" Donna asked, pulling a set of electric clippers from her carrier and plugging them in by the mirror. She'd pulled a stool from under the sink and was sitting down before Rylie had a chance to answer.

"It's on you if I slip and give you a bald spot," Rylie said with a smile, rubbing Donna's short spiky hair with a grin.

"It has a spacer on it, you can't screw it up," Donna assured Rylie as she passed the clippers over her shoulder. "It bothers some of the other girls that I won't let my hair grow out," she said, her eyes locked on Rylie's in the mirror.

"Do they know why?" Rylie asked.

"No, I haven't told anyone in a long time," she said as she closed her eyes. It made Rylie feel oddly special. Donna trusted her.

Rylie switched the clippers on and ran her free hand

through Donna's short hair again. Rylie ran the clippers over Donna's scalp and then alternated, running a hand through her hair to make it stand up before cutting it again. Donna sat with her eyes closed, a contented smile on her face as a fine dusting of clippings fell around her. She rarely went more than three days without cutting her hair. "That was so nice," Donna mumbled when Rylie switched off the clippers.

"Okay, my turn," Rylie said slowly, a smile creeping across her face.

"You sure," Donna asked excitedly, jumping off the stool and grabbing the clippers.

"Absolutely," Rylie said, looking at the unruly mess of hair resting on her shoulders. "Just watch the cut on the back of my head," she said, sitting down and shutting her eyes as she heard the clippers snap to life. Donna moved slowly, being careful not to snag or overload the clippers. After a minute, Rylie sighed and let her shoulders fall forward. Something about the clippers buzzing over her scalp put her into a relaxed stupor.

"You look so good," Donna said when she was done. Rylie squinted, looking at the quarter inch of hair left on her scalp. She ran a hand over her head and smiled. She liked her short hair; she could totally pull it off.

"Should I say you told me all the new girls have to get their heads shaved?"

Donna laughed then got a horrified look on her face. "Sister Kathy would kill me." They broke out in laughter that left them both gasping for air.

They each took a long shower, passing the shampoo over the top of the dividing wall between the stalls and eventually ending up in the TV room watching a silly show about a crazy high school that revolved around music. Rylie couldn't take it seriously, the kids had money and tons of freedom and it just seemed so fake, but she didn't really care, it felt nice to just melt into the cushions and zone. Donna on the other hand was totally engrossed.

When the other girls wandered back in there was a brief flurry of amazed statements as everyone realized Rylie had cut her hair. She might not have done it if she'd known it was going to be an invitation for girls she barely knew to reach out and rub her head. She took it with as much good grace as she could muster. Thankfully it only lasted a few minutes. At nine a buzzer rang and the girls moved back to the dorms and the bathrooms, getting ready for bed. At ten the lights went out.

For Rylie falling asleep the second night was much harder. She was tired and comfortable and should have fallen asleep easily. Instead she tossed and turned, unable to make that final jump away from consciousness and stay there.

She woke up tired, hazy, and wanting nothing more than to pull the covers over her head and go back to sleep. She shut her eyes and tried but Donna didn't stop shaking her until she sat up in her bunk under protest.

Rylie was almost conscious, having just finished breakfast, when Sister Kathy stopped by and asked her to come back to her office. Rylie groaned internally but kept her complaints to herself when Sister Kathy told her she was going to have to take several placement tests to figure out where she was in terms of schooling.

Rylie's morning absolutely sucked. She sat alone in a

room with five number two pencils working her way through a massive skills test which meant endlessly filling out little circles on an answer sheet. Things didn't improve until after lunch. Rylie was called back into Sister Kathy's office and got a surprise visit from Detective Parker. Parker was in her detective clothes, wearing a dark pair of slacks and a suit jacket to hide her firearm from casual observance.

"Hey there," Parker said with a bit of surprise in her voice. The words ended in a grunt as Rylie grabbed Parker and gave her a quick hug. Donna was really rubbing off on her. Rylie stepped back, embarrassed. The hug had been an instant reaction to seeing Parker. She'd secretly wondered if she'd ever see her savior again. How could she ever repay the woman who had kept her out of Ten Acres? The embarrassment she felt only lasted until she saw the look on Parker's face. The detective was all smiles. "I like the haircut," Parker said, nodding her head.

"Thanks," Rylie said happily, excited and nervous at the same time. Seeing Parker was such an unexpected bonus. "It was spur of the moment."

"Sister Kathy left me a message yesterday telling me how well you were doing," Parker said, holding out a department store bag. "I thought you deserved a present."

"I don't know what to say," Rylie said, her voice choking up as she took out several shirts, two more pairs of jeans, packages of socks and underwear, and a new pair of shoes. "I'm not used to someone being so nice to me," she said honestly, her voice thick with emotion.

"Something tells me you're worth it," Parker said, putting a hand on Rylie's shoulder. "Just remember someday to help someone else and we'll call it even," Parker said, squeezing Rylie's shoulder as they held each other's eyes. Rylie nodded.

Parker couldn't stay long, she was on her lunch break. Rylie felt a little stab in her chest when Parker had to leave. She gave Parker another quick hug before the detective followed Sister Kathy back to the rear entrance.

When Sister Kathy came back into her office Rylie was sitting in the chair across from her desk, wiping tears from her eyes. "I'm sorry, I just needed a second," Rylie said, trying to stop the emotions that were raging through her.

"Take all the time you need. You're safe here. It's okay to let it out," Sister Kathy said, looking at Rylie with nothing but compassion.

"Thank you," Rylie said, "I'm not used to someone being so nice to me. Am I like the hundredth girl Parker's brought you?" she asked idly, wiping her nose on the back of her hand.

"No," Sister Kathy said, a brief look of surprise on her face which she quickly hid. "Parker has always stayed close to us after she graduated, but you are the first girl she has ever brought to us." The words brought fresh tears streaming down Rylie's face.

"Thank you for what you did for Parker," Rylie said, trying to reign in her emotions.

"I believe it is why I was put here," Sister Kathy said.

It took Rylie several long minutes to compose herself enough to go back to her testing. She blew through two pages of questions before the excitement of seeing Parker wore off. Then it became a mind-numbing battle to read each question and fill in the little circles. The afternoon dragged on. When Sister Ida came in and told Rylie she was done for the day she couldn't even remember the last few questions she'd answered. Some of the questions were super easy, others were so complicated Rylie wasn't sure if they were made up.

She had an hour break before dinner. She took a nap on the couch in the TV room, not waking up until Donna poked her so she wouldn't miss dinner. Rylie thanked Donna grumpily. She wasn't used to keeping a schedule. She normally slept until she woke up.

"You don't mind working in the church again after dinner do you?" Donna asked quietly as they ate.

"I don't mind staying here by myself if you want to go out with the girls," Rylie said, looking at all the food on her plate and wondering if she was going to have to watch what she ate. She wasn't used to having regular meals either.

"Think of it as you getting me out of outdoor sports I don't really want to do," Donna said hopefully.

"In that case, you have a partner," Rylie said, putting a mouthful of mashed potatoes in her mouth.

Chapter 8

"Rylie, just a moment," Sister Ida said as the girls of Saint Mary's began to disperse after dinner cleanup was completed. "I have some personal supplies to give you on my desk," she said more quietly when Rylie was closer. "Why don't you go grab them and put them in your dresser and meet us in the church?" the sister suggested.

"I'll try not to clean everything before you get there," Donna said, giving Rylie a little wave as she headed for the church.

Rylie found the plastic bag right where Sister Ida had left it. She took the bag back to her dorm and unpacked two bras, soap, a shower caddy, pads and tampons, nail clippers, and a comb which she really didn't need at the moment. Rylie smiled as she put the things away. It felt good to have belongings. It made Saint Mary's seem more real, more permanent.

Her footsteps echoed in the empty halls as she made her way to the church. The other girls had already left to play softball, leaving the school quiet and deserted. The access door into the church was open when she got there. Rylie made her way through the storage area and almost walked into the church proper before Donna's voice stopped her.

"Oh," Donna moaned, her voice deep and husky. Rylie hugged the wall, putting a hand to her mouth to keep herself from giggling. Rylie peeked around the edge of the entry and saw a solid looking fellow in dark clothing and a motorcycle jacket sitting on the altar stairs. He was turned just far enough away from Rylie that she couldn't see his face. Donna was sitting on his lap, her head tilted back as he kissed her neck and slid one hand over her breasts.

"You shouldn't have cut your hair," the man said, his voice low and deep. "Women should have long hair," he said into Donna's neck.

Rylie started to creep away from the corner, figuring she'd give Donna alone time with her boyfriend who must have returned from wherever the Marines had sent him. It felt wrong to watch them in what was clearly an intimate moment. Rylie was inching back towards the door to the school when she froze.

Something was wrong.

The tingle in her belly which had saved her from trouble hundreds of times was so strong she felt like she might lose the dinner she'd just eaten. Rylie turned back to the church and moved as softly as she could, trying to figure out what was setting off her internal alarms. Her eyebrows furrowed, running through the conversations she'd had with Donna in her head.

Her ears had heard it, it just took her brain a little longer to catch up. Donna had been clipping her hair for a very long time. Her Marine boyfriend would have known that. He likely wouldn't have ever seen her with anything but a buzz cut.

So, who was in the church with Donna? Rylie moved back to the entry into the church and peeked around the edge just as the man began speaking again.

"Did the homeless man give you anything before he was hit by the bus?" the man asked Donna.

"No," Donna said, her voice slurred as if she'd been drugged. Even so, her answer was less than confident.

"Did he give you anything?" the man asked again, this time his tone sharper, more demanding.

"No," Donna repeated, her voice stronger, but quivering with uncertainty. The man paused for a moment, looking down at her before pulling Donna into another embrace. His body blocked Rylie's full view, but she knew in her gut something was wrong, very wrong. As the man loosened his embrace, Donna's arms slid down to hang limply at her sides.

"You were one of the lucky ones," the man said, taking Donna's face in the palm of his hand before driving her body backward to slam her skull into the stair behind them. There was a wet crunching noise and Donna's legs kicked spastically, her heels striking the floor in a little flutter of motion before going still.

Rylie pulled back, leaning against the wall to stay upright. Her body felt numb and far away, as if she were floating above herself. She wanted to run, to hide, but her brain just kept replaying the scene in her head. Donna's skull being smashed into a marble stair.

Rylie heard the thump of Donna's body hit the floor as the man stood up. The sound broke the loop replaying in her head. Her survival instincts were strong. She needed to move. To flee. She swung her head back to the school. Her vision narrowed, locked on the door to the school and the long hallway that stretched out in front of her. What had seemed like a long walk from the dorms now seemed like an insurmountable distance.

She tried to move like a mouse. Sound was her enemy. The church was very quiet. She took one step, then the next, trying not to make any noise. She couldn't stop thinking about Donna. The sound of Donna's skull being crushed played over and over in her ears.

Rylie wanted to curl up on the floor and cry.

Instead, she forced herself to put one foot in front of the other, fighting back the panicked terror that wanted to steal her will to move. She succeeded, for a time, then multiple broken bits of data aligned in her head, and a picture formed, a picture she didn't really want to see. She saw newspaper articles and bits of news she'd seen fly in front of her eyes. Crushed skulls. Strange wounds. The Red Summer Killer. It didn't make any sense though. Why had the Red Summer Killer come to Saint Mary's? The thought nearly cost Rylie control over her bladder. She didn't really understand how or why, but she knew he was there for her.

Her chest was burning. She was so scared she was holding her breath. She needed air. She opened her mouth and her ribs expanded greedily.

In the quiet, the sound was loud and ragged.

"Oh, who do we have there?" the Killer called out softly. "Just stay put, I'll come to you," he promised, his voice a dark purr that turned Rylie's stomach. The man sounded so satisfied, happy, and worst of all, expectant. His fun wasn't quite over yet. "Stay where you are," he commanded, the purr turning sharp and hard. Rylie felt the expectation in his words. He wanted her to stand there and wait, he expected to be obeyed. How could someone's voice be so demanding, so compelling?

There was no way she was going to stand there and let herself be murdered.

Rylie pushed off the wall and ran, sucking in air in ragged gasps as she pumped her legs, moving as fast as she could. She turned at the door to the school, looking back. The Killer walked around the corner she'd just been hiding at and paused, a look of genuine shock on his face. He looked at Rylie with puzzlement as she slammed the door between the church and the school and turned the dead bolt.

It didn't make Rylie feel any safer.

She ran into the main hallway and skidded to a halt, her shoes squeaking on the floor. The closest door to the outside was to her right, but it was the door by the Sister's offices and was always locked. She sprinted the other way and veered into the gymnasium dining hall. She jumped as the first loud bang echoed through the school. It sounded like the Killer had found a sledge hammer to attack the door.

Rylie ran for the kitchen. The sound of squealing metal echoed through the school as she ran to the serving window and jumped, skidding across the stainless steel and landing inside the kitchen. She looked around, not sure what she'd been expecting. The kitchen was a single long room with prep areas, a stove, and a large flat top griddle. At the very end of the kitchen, off to her left, was a wide door with a sign on it that said: DELIVERIES ONLY. She ran for the door, passing the industrial stove tops and a massive pot of boiling water to reach the delivery door.

She came to a jolting stop as her body hit the door. It was locked.

"I'm coming for you, stay where you are" the Killer's voice boomed. He was inside the school.

Rylie turned with wide eyes and swallowed hard. There was nowhere to run. She felt a wave of suffocating calm about to crash over her. She'd felt it just before her mother died. It was a disturbing mix of tranquility and resignation. On some level, she knew it was a survival mechanism, a way to accept catastrophe. She just wasn't ready to stop fighting yet. She wasn't ready to die. She turned and slammed her hands into the delivery door, using the pain to push away the calm. The Killer had taken Donna, now he was coming for her. She was not going to go without a struggle.

"Wait for me," the Killer called out, his voice almost playful. The words slipped into Rylie's skull with oily tendrils, lying to her, telling her the pain and fear would all be over if she just stopped and waited for him. Rylie turned to look, expecting to see the Killer right behind her. He wasn't there – yet. She grabbed her ears, jamming her fists against her head as he called out again. "Wait for me." Each time he spoke she felt the words growing heavier, locking her feet to the floor. His voice was like a drug and each time he spoke a part of Rylie wanted him to continue, to tell her what he wanted. It felt wrong, but the voice was wrapped around her skull, telling her to be still, to wait.

She gritted her teeth and concentrated, grinding her knuckles into her temples. Her body tilted backwards until she was on her heels, about to tip. Rylie let it happen, not trying to correct her balance as she fell backwards into the delivery door. The first thing to make contact with the door was the back of her head. There was a beautiful explosion of pain as the just barely closed wound on the back of her head split open. It was enough.

"Fuck, fuck, fuck," Rylie cursed. The pain was a blessed spark. She wasn't going to give in to fear, to the Killer telling her to be still. She wasn't going to curl into a ball and hide or stand still and let the Killer take her. She was going to fight. She screamed a wordless cry and kicked off the door, knowing she didn't have much time. She slammed the fire alarm near the stove as she bolted to the other end of the kitchen. Rylie smiled to herself as the air filled with the piercing alarm, she'd just made things just a little more even between her and her assailant. Now he was up against a deadline. She just had to survive until the fire trucks showed up.

Rylie could hear the Killer coming as she worked frantically. She jumped when he slammed a door just outside the cafeteria. He must have gone to the dorms first. She worked faster, time was running out.

When the Killer walked into the gym she was standing just behind the serving window, her hands pressed to the stainless-steel countertop to keep them from shaking. The Red Summer Killer looked so normal. He was a well-built man with dark hair. He wasn't what she was expecting at all. He didn't look like a crazed murderer. He looked like anyone you might pass on the street. Then he opened his mouth and spoke.

"None of this will matter soon, I'm almost tempted to let you live, to let you know true suffering. It probably doesn't even matter if you have my wallet at this point, but you can never be too safe" he said with a shrug, his eyes locking on hers. As he spoke something strange happened to his face. Rylie blinked and tilted her head to the right as if that would help her focus. For a moment, she saw the monster in front of her, then it was gone. She was so scared she wasn't sure if she was imagining things or not.

"Real tough coming after teenage girls," Rylie said, stepping back carefully, her voice only cracking once. "I guess hobos and kids are just about as much as you can handle." She regretted the words even as they had their intended effect. The Killer broke into a run, crossing the distance between them in a sprint. He was fast. Rylie stepped carefully to the right just as he put a hand on the edge of the countertop and vaulted inside, an angry sneer on his face. His fingertips brushed her shoulder as he vaulted through the serving window.

He landed on the ground and wiped out, screaming as his legs slid out from under him and he flailed on the floor. Rylie backed away, panting, sweat running down her face as his screams turned from uncontrolled agony to structured cries. From outside the window he'd been unable to see the cardboard boxes she'd spiked through with every kitchen knife and serving fork she could find. His legs, thighs, and one of his arms had all caught the sharp ends of multiple kitchen utensils as he slid out on the cardboard and fell into her trap.

The Killer grabbed the inside edge of the serving counter, slowing pulling himself to his feet as he cursed in something that sounded like Russian or Arabic to Rylie.

"No," Rylie said, panting as the Killer came fully to his feet, ignoring the knives speared into his body. Blood trickled from the bottom of his trousers to puddle around his shoes.

"You," he barked, grabbing one of the knives in his upper thigh, "will pay," he promised, pulling the knife free with a grunt. He dropped the blade and took a small determined step, his face coloring in pain and anger as he inched closer to Rylie.

"If you can catch me," she said, swallowing hard, backing away from him as he inched forward, trying to keep him just out of reach and focused on closing the distance. His fingers were touching her shoulder when she grabbed the handle of the large pot of boiling water and pulled it into the space between them, catching his side in a wave of steaming water and chunks of boiled potatoes.

The Killer screamed, trying to back away only to find his legs unsteady beneath him. He fell to the floor, flopping around as he yowled in pain. Steam filled the air as the boiling water turned red with blood. The Killer's screams tore at Rylie's skull as he climbed onto his hands and knees, ignoring the knives he drove further into his lower legs in the process. Rylie tried not to look at his face, at the way his jaw was clenched, bulging, and the way his teeth filled his mouth. Fear was twisting everything she saw, making it worse. No man's face had ever held so much hate and anger, or so many sharpened teeth.

Rylie put one hand on the counter to her left and used his back as a stepping stone to jump over his body, ignoring the sound of snapping teeth as she landed on his opposite side in a splash of bloody water. She took three steps to the serving window and flew over it, racing away as the Killer screamed in rage behind her.

Rylie ran into the hallway and froze. The Killer was hurt, and badly, but she wasn't ready to declare herself the winner just yet. She didn't get to watch a lot of television, but she'd seen enough to understand the bad guy always got back up once you thought they were down for the count. It was time to hide. She wanted to put a locked door between her and the Killer, but there were no locks on the dorms and the only locks in the bathrooms were lightweight sliders on the stall doors. Rylie ran for the only door she was sure had a lock on it. A thrill ran through her when she reached the end of the hallway and saw

Sister Kathy's office door was open. She ran inside, peeked back to make sure there was no one in the hallway behind her and then carefully shut the door and locked it as quietly as she could.

Rylie turned the light off and felt her away around the desk until she could climb under it and pull the chair as tightly against her as she could, huddling in the corner under the desk, willing herself to be invisible. Her chest heaved, pushing against her knees as she struggled to control her breathing. It was time to be as quiet as a mouse. It wasn't easy. As the adrenaline wore off she began to shake.

Time stretched.

Moments felt like hours.

The fire alarm droned on and on.

She told herself over and over the Killer had to be down. There was no way he could have gotten up and followed her half way across the school bleeding like a stuck pig. The growing sound of sirens and the air horns of fire trucks was the sweetest music she'd ever heard. She bit back a scream when she heard the door to the office shake, every muscle in her body tensing. She heard a male voice saying something. She was so scared she couldn't make sense of the words.

A man's voice was demanding that if anyone were in the room they should unlock the door. Rylie didn't move. When the door was kicked in she began screaming, then hit her head as she tried to surge to her feet while still under the desk. When she managed to stand up she grabbed a pencil from the desk, screaming in anger, ready to attack.

The fireman paused, putting his hands up, his mouth

moving and making words she did not hear as she brandished a number two pencil at him. "It's okay," the fireman said over and over until the words finally reached Rylie's brain. She dropped the pencil and fell onto the desk crying and shaking.

Rylie was still crying when Sister Kathy came in with a medic. The sister helped guide Rylie out into the hallway where the paramedic guided her onto a stretcher. Rylie grabbed Sister Kathy's shoulders, "He killed Donna." The words sounded unreal, even though she was the one saying them. Sister Kathy nodded, tears sliding down her cheeks as she did her best to comfort Rylie through her own grief. Rylie continued to blubber. Her friend was dead.

Time slipped for Rylie. She was inside with Sister Kathy, then she was in an ambulance, the back of the stretcher angled up so she could see out the rear of the vehicle. The paramedic worked, telling Rylie over and over that she was safe. They were going to take care of her. It was something he'd clearly said many times, on many nights. As he spoke he ran his hands over Rylie's legs, looking for wounds. Her lower legs were covered in blood. The paramedic had no way of knowing who's it was.

"I'm okay, it's not mine" Rylie croaked. As soon as she said the words she thought about the Killer, and then about Donna. She started sobbing and crying again.

"You're safe now," the paramedic repeated, carefully examining her scalp. The back of her shirt was stained red, and that was her own blood.

"Do you have a cell phone?" Rylie asked, reaching into her back pocket until she found what she was looking for. She'd kept Parker's card with her since the moment she'd gotten to Saint

Mary's.

"Yes," the paramedic answered cautiously.

She pulled the card from her pocket and handed it to him. "Please call her," she begged, using her shirt to wipe her nose. Whenever she cried her nose ran. The paramedic looked at the card and frowned.

"The police are already here," he said, nodding to uniformed figures standing in front of the ambulance.

"Please, call her," Rylie pleaded, keeping her voice low as she begged, her hand grabbing his arm, digging into his flesh.

"Okay," he said, pulling away, still not sounding convinced. He looked at the card for another moment but didn't take out his cell. Instead he grabbed a radio hanging near the front of the ambulance and started to talk to his dispatcher, turning the volume down to its lowest setting as he did so. He asked to be connected to the local police dispatch. There was some radio chatter and then the paramedic was asking for Detective Parker, staring at Rylie as if she might have made the card herself for some nefarious purpose.

"Do you know a girl named Rylie?" the paramedic asked. Rylie couldn't hear the reply. Whatever came back was just a rapid staccato of noise. "No, I got that, I understand," the paramedic said, giving Rylie a strange look as he hung the radio back up.

"She tell you I was gonna run?" Rylie asked as the fellow grabbed a blanket and laid it over Rylie up to her neck.

"No," the paramedic said, lowering his voice. "She told me you were hurt and that no one should see you or talk to you until she got here. So shut your pie hole," he demanded, his eyes looking out the back of the ambulance as he opened packages and started to look busy.

"I'm just shaken up," Rylie said, still dazed and confused from everything that had happened.

"No, you're hurt, you may have to go to the hospital. Now shut up and lay back," he said, half standing to grab something from the cabinet overhead. Someone came to the back of the ambulance, banging on the side of the vehicle to get the paramedics attention. "Give me fifteen okay guys, she banged her head somewhere along the line and I'm not sure if she's got a concussion. Let me get the bleeding stopped and if her pupils are reactive and equal, then she is all yours," the paramedic yelled, sounding tired and overworked as he pushed a wad of gauze to the back of Rylie's head.

The paramedic mumbled to Rylie as he worked. "Your friend just told me if you weren't in this ambulance when she got here she was going to have my head, and she knows my boss, and both his wife and his girlfriend's names, so I don't think she's shitting me. If this comes down on me I'm going to crack your head open even more so none of this was make believe," he whispered in Rylie's ear.

Rylie knew Parker was there before she ever saw her. Parker's car came in hot, skidding to a halt a half second before Parker appeared at the back of the ambulance. She was all business, her face a mask of barely controlled rage as she barked at the two uniformed officers standing a few feet in front of the ambulance. "Guys, I have a priority transport order from the captain," Parker said sharply.

"We were told to hold onto her," one of the uniformed

officers said.

"Move your ass," Parker demanded angrily. "Who do you think you were holding her for? The captain wants to make sure we get a shot at her before the feds take over this case and we lose any chance to get the Red Summer Killer ourselves." The two fellows looked at each other and shrugged, letting Parker climb into the back of the ambulance.

"Can you walk?" Parker asked, her tone hard, devoid of any nicety. Rylie nodded yes, stunned and hurt by Parker's demeanor. It had not been what she was expecting. "Good," Parker said, yanking the blankets off before grabbing Rylie by her arm and dragging her out the back of the ambulance. The paramedic threw the gauze and tape in his hands to the floor and sighed in confused disgust. As Parker pulled Rylie to her car she yelled at the two uniformed officers who were walking away. "What are you doing? Stand here and look like you're guarding something until the feds actually ask to see the witness," she said angrily.

Parker peeled away from Saint Mary's, the rear of the car squirming as she accelerated at a barely controlled pace. "I'm sorry" Rylie said softly, trying to hold off tears. Parker flexed her hands on the wheel, revealing indents where she'd crushed the dense foam. Parker didn't seem to pay any attention to Rylie. She drove fast and aggressively, focused on the road and the cars she was just barely avoiding as she cut people off and ran red lights with little blips of her siren. Each time she turned her siren on the lights embedded under the front and rear windshields would turn on as well. Rylie shut her eyes each time they approached a light. The combination of noise and strobe lights made her feel nauseous.

Parker checked the rear view constantly as she drove, changing lanes and making turns without using her turn signals. Rylie watched her, growing more anxious as Parker continued to focus on the road. Parker appeared to be struggling with something. Her jaw was clenched and her face was flushed. Not the pretty kind of flushed you get from a nice jog either. Parker's face was blotchy and red with veins standing out on her neck and forehead. It was the face of someone lifting something fifty pounds over their safe limit.

"I didn't do anything. I didn't want him to come there" Rylie promised, no longer able to hold the tears back.

Parker looked over at Rylie, her eyes going wide as if she were surprised to see her there before she shook her head and sighed heavily. "I'm sorry Rylie, I know you didn't do anything," she said. She looked behind her one more time before slowing the car to a more reasonable speed. She pursed her lips, breathing very purposefully. "Did you see him?"

"Yes," Rylie said, shaking her head numbly in acknowledgement. "He killed my friend Donna." Tears continued to slide down Rylie's cheeks.

"It doesn't make sense," Parker said, her voice trailing off.

"He," Rylie said, pausing to swallow, "he came for me. I think it had something to do with the old man killed by the bus." Rylie shook her head. It didn't make sense, she just knew it was true. Rylie tried to put it into words. "The homeless guy attacked me, and then the Killer came to Saint Mary's. Somehow it's related. I'm not sure what's going on," Rylie said weakly. She was physically and emotionally exhausted.

"I'm not sure what's going on either," Parker said, trying to be supportive. "I wasn't mad at you when I came to get you, I just had to be a bitch to get the other officers to do what I wanted," she said, reaching out a hand to grab Rylie's.

"I thought I did something wrong," Rylie said, holding Parker's hand with both of hers. Rylie hadn't realized how cold she was until she had Parker's dry, warm hand clutched in hers.

"I'm a little off the reservation here. If I'd let that paramedic or those cops know I was personally invested they might not have listened or let me take you," Parker said, the words spoken softly.

"Thank you," Rylie said, feeling a little lighter. Parker was more than a cop to her.

"What happened? There was a blood trail from the kitchen back to the church, but the responding officers lost the trail one street over," Parker asked, squeezing Rylie's hand.

"I hurt him. I tricked him into jumping through the kitchen window onto knives. I think I hurt him, but not enough if he got away." Rylie said with dread, her voice growing husky as she thought about the Red Summer Killer still being out there.

"I was worried...about you. On the radio on the way to Saint Mary's I heard a lot of radio chatter. The kitchen was soaked with bloody water."

"They were prepping something for tomorrow's meals," Rylie explained. "I pulled a pot of boiling water onto him after he thought he had me cornered."

"You're a tough kid," Parker said, squeezing Rylie's hand again before pulling it away so she could put both hands back on the wheel. The note of respect in her voice made Rylie beam with pride.

They drove in silence for a while, each of them lost in their own private thoughts. "He came to Saint Mary's looking for me," Rylie said slowly, distracted. Now that she was safe the little bits and pieces of the puzzle were settling out, falling into an order that began to make at least a little sense. Rylie kept seeing Donna on the Killer's lap as she walked into the church, the scene wouldn't stop replaying in her head. She stopped trying to fight it and instead let the scene play out, not trying to repress it, and instead accepted the pain while she analyzed each little moment.

"You can't blame yourself for what happened to the other girl," Parker said.

"No, Donna is dead because of me," Rylie said. She was sure of it. The words were hammer blows to her heart.

"It's not your fault, he" Parker began before Rylie cut her off.

"He had Donna on his lap in the church. He told her she shouldn't have cut her hair," Rylie said, forcing the words out even though her throat hurt with pent up emotion. The car swerved as Parker lost her focus, almost clipping the parked cars on their right as she sped down the road.

"He mentioned your hair?" Parker asked, her voice full of anxious disbelief.

"Yes, I think he got us confused," Rylie said, her voice barely audible over the road noise. In her mind, she kept seeing the way Donna's feet jerked as she died. Between the images in her head and the way Parker's Crown Vic swayed on its shocks Rylie was feeling like she was going to puke.

"I thought it was funny," Parker said, shaking her head. Her voice was far away. "I filled out your transport paperwork after I saw you at lunch. I annotated that you had all your hair when I dropped you off and that the head shaving occurred after you were released to Saint Mary's. I didn't even think anyone was going to read it."

"What does it mean?" Rylie asked quietly, not quite understanding what Parker was telling her. Rylie shut her eyes and tried to center herself against the nausea threatening to overwhelm her.

"Nothing good," Parker said, sounding just as shaken as Rylie felt. "My boss, Captain Nowak has had some suspicions that the Red Summer Killer was someone in law enforcement, maybe even someone inside the FBI. It's why my boss wanted me to get you out of there before anyone else showed up," Parker said.

"That's not very comforting," Rylie mumbled, looking out the window as they drove. Parker opened her mouth to say something then closed it. She didn't find it any more comforting than Rylie did and trying to pretend otherwise felt dishonest.

Rylie watched the city go by, not recognizing where they were until she thought she saw the same shopping center twice. Was Parker driving in circles? "Where are we going?" Rylie asked, breaking the silence. Rylie was sure they'd looped back on themselves at least once although she didn't recognize the upscale storefronts they were passing.

"I can't take you back to my apartment. If it is someone in law enforcement it would be too easy to find us there. I called Nowak right after I talked to the paramedic. He told me to keep you safe while he figures out what to do. So, I am taking you someplace no one knows about," she said, slowing down as she turned into an alley behind a row of stores. Car ports jutted off the building at regular intervals, providing sheltered parking for the apartments over the stores. Next to every carport was a set of stairs leading up to a private entry to each apartment.

Parker pulled into an empty carport and turned her cruiser off.

"Where are we?" Rylie asked as she climbed out of the car and Parker guided her up the stairs.

"An ex-boyfriend is out of town for a few weeks. I told him I'd water his plants while he was gone."

"Is he a cop?" Rylie asked as Parker retrieved a key from a plastic rock hiding in a potted plant just outside the door.

"No, he's in software design. It was a very short but intense relationship. No one from work ever met him," Parker said, holding the door open so Rylie could slip inside.

The apartment was stifling. The air smelled of dry grass with a tinge of something not quite so pleasant. The air had been off for days. Parker locked the door behind them and turned on the lights before going straight to the thermostat. There was a brief mechanical noise as the air conditioner turned on. "Sorry, I must have turned it off by accident," she said with a shrug before pulling off her jacket and throwing it over the back of a kitchen chair.

Rylie walked into the kitchen and stopped. The normalcy of the apartment struck her as out of place. How could it look so normal when everything around her had changed so quickly, so badly? She surveyed the open layout of the apartment numbly. It was basically one large room divided into a kitchen and a living room by a small countertop. A door on the far side of the television was partially open, revealing a bedroom. Potted plants sat in every window and a large planter sat on either side of the couch, filled with overflowing fronds. All the plants were brown and dried out.

"Make yourself at home," Parker said, going to the sink to get a glass of water. Rylie went to the couch and collapsed, sinking into the cushions, letting her head fall back gently so she didn't put any pressure on her freshly re-opened wounds. She stared up at the ceiling for a while, trying to lose herself in its textured nothingness. Her hand reached out idly as she zoned and grabbed one of the fronds of the nearest potted plant. It crumbled into pieces as Rylie rubbed it between her thumb and fingers. Rylie turned her head to watch the bits of debris falling to the floor. It looked like ash as it fell.

"He wasn't a good boyfriend," Parker said from the kitchen.

"Guess not," Rylie said, dusting her hand off on the side of the couch. "Is it okay if I watch TV?"

"Yes, of course," Parker said, setting her glass on the counter as she slipped into the living room. She grabbed the remote and turned on the set before handing Rylie the controller. Rylie flipped through the channels until she found something meaningless while Parker disappeared into the bedroom and shut the door. Rylie heard the toilette flush and a few minutes later Parker came out in jeans and a tee. She sat down on the opposite side of the couch and the two of them sat there, staring at the screen.

"Bathroom?" Rylie asked, pointing to the bedroom door as

she climbed to her feet. Parker nodded.

Rylie peed, washed her hands, and then paused, staring at herself in the mirror over the sink. The top of her head was swathed in white cotton. For the second time in less than a week she pulled bandages off her head. The final strip was the worst. She poured water over the back of her head to loosen up the congealed blood. It didn't help. She used the wadded-up bandages to clean up the back of her head before pausing to stare at her short spiky hair in the mirror. Her jaw clenched, bulging as she stared herself down, refusing to let her mind replay Donna's final moments in the church.

Rylie turned away from the mirror, panting, filled with an overpowering urge to run. She wanted to wake up in her nest of blankets hidden away down by the waterfront. She wanted to disappear back onto the streets and forget everything that had happened over the last three days. She looked out the small window over the tub. For a heartbeat the night called to her, whispering that she could still run, disappear. Out in the living room Parker made some noise and it brought Rylie back to reality. The Red Summer Killer had tried to take her life. She had seen his face. There was no way the police, the feds, or Parker for that matter, were going to let her slip away into obscurity.

Rylie figured life couldn't get much worse.

Chapter 9

When Rylie came back into the living room Parker was sitting on the couch directly in front of the television, her butt right on the end of the cushions. She had the remote in one hand, increasing the volume with stabs of her thumb. Parker held up a hand as Rylie walked in, telling Rylie to be quiet before she could even open her mouth. Rylie scurried between Parker and the TV and sat down so she could see what Parker was watching.

The TV screen was filled with the outline of a building against a dull sky. The cameraman on the ground zoomed in on the rooftop, revealing a man standing on the edge of the roof. *"An officer specializing in negotiating has been called to the scene but we have reports the doors to the roof have been locked or blockaded from the outside. For our viewers, this is a live feed and due to the nature of this situation it may not be suitable for children."* The cameraman zoomed in to the limits of his camera, revealing the outline of a man against the darkening night sky, his lower body lit by the lights around the roof of the building. The man was wearing an overflowing bath robe that had seen better days. The edges of the robe were frayed and torn and whipped about in the wind.

"Oh, my god," Parker said as the man's robe was caught in a gust of wind, billowing it around him like a grand cape. As the wind lifted the material the man's chest came into view. Underneath the robe the man was wearing what looked like a suicide vest. The announcer kept talking as a grainy still image was plastered to the upper right corner of the screen showing the vest. The newscaster once again warned viewers about what they were seeing as they cut from the ground camera to a much clearer image taken from the news helicopter which had just come on station. The helicopter was hovering above the high rise, showing the ocean in the distance as the sun disappeared over the horizon.

Parker and Rylie watched in stunned horror as the screen split, showing the rooftop feed from the helicopter on one half of the screen and street level view on the other. The moment the jumper's vest was shown on the television a flurry of activity started. Family and friends began to call and text their loved ones, there was a suicide bomber in downtown. Everyone in a ten block radius poured out onto the streets, jamming together in a confused mix of bodies as everyone tried to go in different directions. The police on the scene were overwhelmed. They tried to direct traffic, to maintain the calm but there were just too many bodies. It was utter chaos.

The newswoman on the ground tried to do her job. She screamed into her microphone, trying to get comments from the people streaming around her until she gave up, letting her microphone drop to her side as she stood, watching the press of bodies streaming by. Twice the newswoman was almost swept away in the stream of fleeing pedestrians, and twice a large hairy arm shot out and grabbed her as the camera's view swung wide. After the second time the newswoman thanked her cameraman and retreated from view to stand against the back of the news van. Her cameraman stood next to her, continuing to film the press of bodies moving in every direction.

A male voice cut in, thanking the newswoman and telling

her to be safe as her audio was cut off and the screen format shifted again. The street view and the helicopter shot of the rooftop shrank to fill the upper right and left quadrants of the screen while the lower half became a shot of a panel of terrorism experts sitting around a curved table. Parker turned the volume down as the experts began to throw out wild speculations about the jumper and his possible motivations.

"This is real, right?" Rylie asked. She had already been through a lot and wasn't sure if she could trust her own eyes. Too many things were happening around her.

"Yes," Parker said sadly, not taking her eyes off the TV. A scroll at the bottom of the screen cycled over and over. "**This broadcast is suitable for mature audiences only.**" The rooftop filled the screen again as the helicopter positioned itself to get a better view of the top of the building. Parker sucked a breath in as they watched the SWAT team kick open the door to the roof. Rylie and Parker watched tensely as the SWAT team closed the distance to the man standing on the edge of the roof. "They will try to talk him down," Parker said quietly, speaking more to herself than to Rylie. Rylie looked at the digital clock on the cable box just as the hour turned.

The numbers flashed nine - zero - zero just before the man stepped off the roof. The camera followed the jumper as he fell while at the same time a loud clear voice cut through the chatter on the television. "Cut away, cut away," the producer was screaming. "Holy shit," the same voice said as the man exploded four seconds into his fall. One moment the camera crew in the helicopter was tracking the jumper as he fell and then there was a flash of brightness and his body disappeared in a flash of light.

Whoever was controlling the feeds was too slow to keep the live audience from seeing the body come apart in midair. Producers were yelling for the feed to cut back to the newsroom as the helicopter veered away from downtown, filling the screen with the horizon as it banked and turned.

The male producer's voice was cut off midway through a sentence as the screen shifted first to the terrorism panel where one of the female experts was looking at her phone and crying as she tried to call someone – then back to the ground crew. The female anchor and her cameraman were still at street level, but they had retreated into their news van, filming out of the open rear doors. The anchor was kneeling to one side, not realizing she was on live as she held her microphone clutched in both hands.

"Suzy, can you tell us what is going on?" The newsroom was trying to get Suzy's attention.

When Suzy realized she was on live her eyes went wide in surprise, but she was an experienced newscaster and recovered quickly. "As you can see we've retreated into the news van for safety," Suzie said loudly into her microphone. "We heard the explosion above us and it sounded like some shrapnel hit the van and the buildings around us but we don't know if anyone on the ground has been hurt." She leaned back against the van wall as the cameraman panned the street.

"What is that?" Rylie wondered aloud, staring at the image as what looked like a fine mist descended from above. The cameraman focused on the mist as it settled on the clean glass of the building across from them. The mist settled in fine little drops that slowly trickled down the glass in dark droplets. The interior lights behind the glass caught the streaks, shining through them, showing their dark ruby color.

"Blood," Parker whispered, not wanting to say the word.

"What the fuck?" Suzie said quizzically, not realizing or caring if her mic was still live. The cameraman snapped his fingers twice as he zoomed out, bringing Suzie back into view. She settled herself with a deep breath, ignored her last comment, and forced herself to speak. She pointed to the road behind her as she spoke, "Hopefully the police and emergency response teams will soon have the situation here under control. We still don't know if anyone on the ground has been hurt," she continued as her cameraman climbed forward so he could get a better view around them.

When the explosion went off everyone dove for whatever cover they could find. People were lying on the street or huddled behind cars and crammed into entryways, anywhere there was a bit of potential protection. The camera was rolling as the shock wore off and people began to stir. Parker and Riley watched as peopled struggled to their feet.

"Something is wrong," Parker said.

"No shit," Riley agreed, neither of them took their eyes off the television.

The sound of a gunshot from the television kept Parker from saying anything else. On the television the female anchor babbled about the importance of staying calm as the cameraman hung out the van door, looking up the street to their right. When the camera stabilized, the screen showed two businessmen attacking a uniformed cop. The businessmen were trying to close on the officer, reaching out for him, trying to get a hold of him. The cop stumbled and lost his footing as he tried to backpedal. It was a costly mistake, the moment he began to fall the two businessmen were on him. The cop did the only thing he could and fired more shots at point blank range.

"How did he miss?" Riley asked as the three bodies wrestled on the ground.

The cameraman hesitated, then climbed halfway out of the van so he could get a better shot. The image wobbled as the cameraman struggled with whether he should put his camera down and go help the cop. Before he could make up his mind one of the two businessmen lifted his head with a savage yank. Blood sprayed up from beneath the businessman, a red spurting jet arcing through the air as his jaws snapped up the meat hanging from his teeth.

"Holy shit," the cameraman said in shock. The screen was filled with a close in view of the cop, still struggling beneath his two attackers. The cameraman was running on instinct, zooming in as the cop jammed his revolver up under the blood-stained chin of the businessman on top of the pile and pulled the trigger. A volcano of gore erupted from the top of the businessman's head a half second before the control room cut the live feed and shifted back to the news room.

A shaken anchor did his best to apologize to the viewers as the audio from the ground crew and the newsroom combined. The senior board operator had stood up from his chair and left when he saw the explosion. He lived four blocks from downtown and his wife and child were there. Work was no longer his priority. The junior board operator had been a co-op for the last year but had very little actual experience. The anchor in the news room tried to raise his voice over the sound of more gunshots and screaming coming in from the live feed.

The anchor in the newsroom continued to yell into his microphone even after the junior board operator figured out how to turn off the audio from the news van. When the anchor switched back to his normal voice he was covered in sweat, asking the producer in the control booth if they were able to get any updates from the San Diego police. No one answered him, the producer was too busy trying to make sure the junior board operator knew what buttons and slides to push.

The lead anchor continued to apologize. He was pale and sweating and every few moments he would look up to where he knew the producer should be watching him from the control room and glare before continuing to speak. He wanted them to cut away, to do anything but stay on him. He didn't have any information, he was rattled. He didn't know what to say. He had no way of knowing that half the staff in the control room had stepped out to call loved ones or outright abandoned their posts.

Parker lifted the remote, about to change the channel when the female weather anchor walked over and handed the lead a piece of paper. No one left in the control room knew how to feed the teleprompter. The anchor glanced between the paper and the camera as he spoke. "**There has been a coordinated terrorist attack on our great city. The police are asking everyone to stay inside and stay calm. If you are hurt, please call emergency services. There have been several explosions near and around downtown and the mayor has declared a state of emergency.**"

"Do you need to do something?" Rylie asked nervously,

turning to Parker.

Parker pulled out her cell phone and looked at the black screen, her finger on the power button. Rylie watched as Parker's thumb twitched over so slightly. "I don't think so," Parker said shakily, still staring at the phone. "No, he told me to keep you safe, I can't leave you alone," Parker said more firmly, setting her phone down on the coffee table with more force than was necessary. Rylie tried to hide her sigh of relief. A part of her had been afraid Parker would have to go.

Parker scanned the news channels, listening to bits and pieces, waiting for someone to say something new. Each channel was struggling to deal with a rapidly evolving story. They heard the same announcement several more times as the official message hit each station. Parker was flipping through the channels when an anchor said, "**This content is extremely graphic, you have been warned,**" and paused her thumb. The screen cut to a shaky cell phone video taken through what looked like the rear window of a delivery van. Two men wearing aprons were guarding the front of a butcher's shop. They were clearly related. If it weren't for the two decades of age difference between the father and son, they would have looked like twins.

A woman wearing jeans was the first to come running into frame. She ran directly for the older man on the right and leapt at him without hesitation. The bat in the man's hands had barely been visible until he was swinging it. The blow struck her in the air, hitting her in the side of the head with crushing force that redirected her momentum, sending her into the glass storefront with enough energy to make the glass flex from the impact. Her crushed head left a bloody smear on the glass as she fell.

Within seconds the men were rushed again. Four teenage boys attacked and went down in a brutal melee of swinging bats. The two men looked at each other and decided they'd had enough. They fled back into their store and locked the doors just in time to stop a mailman who ran headlong into the entry only to bounce back two steps when he hit the glass. The impact barely slowed the mailman, he came right back at the door, hammering his fists into the glass in rage. The activity attracted others. In ones and twos, a horde formed until the front of the butcher's shop was completely obscured by angry bodies that pushed and shoved, trying to get to the front.

The hand holding the cell phone was shaking, making it hard to see exactly what was happening. One moment there was a mass of bodies fighting at the front doors of the butcher shop, and then the glass over their heads popped, going opaque as it broke into thousands of pieces and bodies surged into the shop.

The view shifted quickly as the person holding the cell phone crawled away from the rear window of the van. The news station cut away from the video just as a bloody hand slammed against the glass, leaving a bloody handprint as it pulled away. The three anchors sitting behind their curved futuristic desk looked pale and their voices were subdued as they began to interview a terrorism expert via satellite link.

Everyone was spouting theories. State sponsored terror, some form of biologic agent release, hysteria driving people to riot. Parker listened to a few theories before continuing to channel surf. She didn't know what she was looking for, but she figured she'd know it if she saw it. After another five minutes of listening to pundits trying to make sense of what was going on Parker stood up and went into the bedroom to grab her car keys. Things weren't normalizing, the situation was getting worse, spreading across the city.

"I'll be right back," she told Rylie, who followed her to the apartment door. The moment Parker opened the door the sound of distant sirens and gunshots hit them both. "This will just take a second," Parker promised, stepping outside before moving quickly down the steps. Parker was only out of sight for fifteen seconds when she was beneath the carport, but Rylie was still filled with relief when Parker came back into view, her arms loaded down with gear. Rylie stepped back, holding the door open so Parker could get through before immediately slamming it closed and locking it.

Parker spread her gear out on the kitchen table, organizing it as she took a mental inventory. Rylie stood to the side and watched as Parker touched each item, making sure she had everything she'd gone to retrieve. The biggest item was a long black nylon gun case. The assorted smaller items were clear plastic boxes filled with shotgun and pistol ammo, a flashlight, cuffs, extra magazines, and a spring-loaded police baton.

"What's all this?" Rylie asked, looking at the gear skeptically.

"I felt safer having this inside," Parker said, unzipping the nylon gun case and sliding a shotgun free, a hint of a smile touching her lips. Parker unclipped the bungee sling before dropping the elastic strap on the table. Rylie pulled up a chair on the other side of the kitchen table, watching in fascination as Parker disassembled the weapon. There was something very close to a ritual in the way Parker's hands moved. She put her finger into the loading port before racking the slide. Rylie watched Parker unloaded the shotgun one shell at a time, lining them up on the table. After unloading the shotgun, Parker pulled the pump back and double checked the weapon was clear. She saw Rylie watching and smiled. "Sorry, it helps me relax," she said as she unscrewed the magazine cap and slid the barrel off the weapon.

"Sure..." Rylie said, nodding her head as if that made perfect sense, "...relaxing."

"The last time I had this shotgun out of the trunk was over a year ago, I just want to make sure it's in good shape," Parker said as she put her fingers into the receiver and pulled forward on the slide until it came free, carrying a hunk of cylindrical metal out of the heart of the gun. "This is a Remington 870 tactical shotgun," Parker continued as she set the parts down and inspected them. "I wish I had some gun oil, but I sprayed her down with oil before I put her in my trunk," she said mostly to herself. Rylie watched as Parker's fingers re-assembled the weapon quickly and efficiently. It was something Parker had clearly done many times before.

Rylie pointed at one of the shells sitting on the table and waited for Parker to give her an approving nod before picking it up. "That is a twelve gauge, one ounce slug," Parker said as Rylie looked at the big chunk of rounded lead that sat flush with the end of the blue plastic hull. "It will stop just about anything it hits," Parker said.

"I've never touched a bullet before," Rylie said, feeling the weight of the shotgun shell in her hand.

The edges of Parker's mouth pulled up in a smile. "That's technically a shell. Shotguns use shells. Bullets have metal casings," she explained, grabbing one of her spare clips and popping a round free. She handed it to Rylie. Rylie looked at both projectiles. The handgun round looked tiny and elegant in comparison to the shotgun shell.

"You're so comfortable with this stuff," Rylie said, watching Parker reassemble the shotgun quickly and efficiently. Rylie set the shotgun shell and the handgun round on the table carefully so they were both standing up.

"It comes from spending a lot of time shooting them and cleaning them. Guns are tools just like any other," Parker said. "Respect them and take care of them and they become like an extension of your hands," she said, standing up with the shotgun in her hands. "Come here," Parker said, motioning for Rylie to come over.

Rylie stood up, surprised when Parker held the shotgun out for her to take. Rylie stopped, looking at the shotgun, then at Parker, unsure. She'd never touched a firearm before. 'It's okay, just never touch a weapon unless you are with me," Parker said, holding the shotgun out further for Rylie to take.

Rylie took the weapon tentatively, surprised at its weight. She was careful to keep it pointed at the ceiling, for some reason thinking this would keep anything bad from happening. "First thing, you always make sure the weapon is unloaded," Parker said, looking at Rylie expectantly.

Rylie tried to repeat what she'd seen Parker do, but when she tried to pull the pump back it wouldn't budge. Parker turned the weapon in Rylie's hands so she could see the little lever just in front of the trigger. Rylie pushed it and the slide immediately moved to the rear. "Now you check two things, the first is that there is no round in the chamber," Parker said, pointing to where the shell would sit if it were chambered. "The next thing you do is make sure there is nothing in the magazine. See that orange circle," she said, pointing through the loading port at the tube under the chamber. Rylie nodded. "That is the follower. If you can see the orange, you know there are no shells in the magazine tube. The weapon is clear," she said.

"Close it?" Rylie asked, feeling a little more comfortable now that she was sure the weapon was unloaded. Parker nodded and Rylie racked the slide, locking the weapon into its firing position.

"Now put it to your shoulder," Parker said, slipping around Rylie as she brought the shotgun up. Parker's arms wrapped around Rylie, pulling the shotgun tight to her shoulder. "Keep your head down, you want to put the bead at the end of the weapon in the middle of the ring on top of the receiver. Rylie lowered her head and looked down the barrel, lining the little metallic bead on the front of the weapon inside the ring on top of the receiver just as Parker had told her.

"Oh," Rylie said, jumping as Parker shifted her grip, grabbing her by the hips.

"Sorry," Parker said, pulling back quickly.

"No, it's okay, keep going," Rylie said. "You just surprised me."

"Okay," Parker said, tilting Rylie's hips before changing her hand position again, putting a finger though a belt loop of Rylie's jeans while also pushing Rylie's shoulder blades forward with a hand in the middle of her back. "You have to lean into it, you want your shoulders in front of your hips so the recoil doesn't throw you off balance," Parker said, stepping back to look at Rylie's form.

For just a moment the two of them were lost in the moment. Rylie turned and smiled at Parker, handing her the weapon with the barrel pointed up. Parker, smiled and took the shotgun before her face went blank. She shook her head and sighed heavily while pinching her eyes closed with one hand while she held the weapon with the other. "I just let a minor, and a witness, handle a police issued shotgun," Parker said to herself, setting the weapon on the counter before rubbing her temples.

"I won't tell anyone," Rylie promised. Parker laughed weakly. "You are a good teacher, it took both our minds off what's going on," Rylie said, trying again.

"Thank you, Rylie," Parker said, letting just a hint of a smile touch her face. "Promise me you won't touch any of the weapons unless I tell you it's okay?" Rylie nodded her head in agreement but Parker still looked like she was wondering if she'd just made a huge mistake.

"I promise I won't touch the guns," Rylie said, her eyes locked on Parkers for a long moment before she stuck her tongue out.

"Okay, I believe you," Parker said, rolling her eyes at Rylie playfully. She set the shotgun on the counter and went back to the living room couch. Several pundits were arguing over the mayor's declaration of emergency and the curfew that went with it. Even in the face of what was turning into a large scale riot, politics were being played. One pundit wondered if the mayor would face lawsuits after declaring martial law while another wondered if he'd face civil suits for not doing it soon enough.

"Vultures," Parker said as she settled back into the couch. Rylie sat down next to her. Parker changed news stations until she found one with a live feed of downtown. It took them both a moment to orient themselves to what they were seeing. A helicopter was flying above downtown, tracking what appeared to be a large mob moving through the streets. As the helicopter followed the mob a newscasters said it was the worst violence he'd ever seen, and he'd been on the streets during the 1992 Los Angeles riots. He warned the viewers that most of the police dispatch numbers were overloaded and to stay inside and not open their doors for anyone. Whatever was raging through the city was infectious and spreading. The newsroom took that moment to show a shaky cell phone video of what looked to be a senior police official yelling into his cell phone, screaming for CDC support and federal aid. He used the words biological attack seven times in a sixty second rant.

"Do you know him?" Rylie asked as the news churned on.

"Not personally, he's the Deputy Commissioner, so he's my boss's, boss's, boss, or something like that. Whoever took that video better hope the Commissioner doesn't find him," Parker said, shaking her head as the news continued on.

"This isn't normal," Rylie said, her voice soft, hushed by fear and confusion. There was no good news on the television. The situation continued to grow out of control.

"I'll keep you safe," Parker said, putting a hand out to squeeze Rylie's thigh, her eyes never leaving the television. Rylie nodded, wanting to believe her. She watched Parker and the news at the same time. Every time a police officer was shown onscreen Rylie noticed how Parker looked at her cell phone where it sat with a dark screen on the coffee table. Rylie was afraid that if Parker turned the phone on she was going to get called in. That put a knot in Rylie's stomach, and not just for selfish reasons. People were dying in the streets, and cops weren't immune to whatever was going down. Of course, the thought of being left alone in the apartment if Parker did leave wasn't comforting either.

The news stations had learned their lessons about the dangers of live feeds. Instead of showing the raw carnage they played snippets of heavily edited footage. Rylie couldn't decide what was worse, seeing the raw footage or having it pixelated out. Whenever she saw the pixilation her mind just filled in the blanks, sometimes with more detail than was necessary.

Parker was flipping through news channels when they all cut to the emergency broadcast system. The screen showed multi colored bars as the speakers cut loose with a suitably annoying tone before the Governor of California filled the screen. The Governor was a soap opera star turned politician, a middle-aged hopeful trying to become the next Ronal Reagan. He was known for being calm and collected, a man with a quick wit who was never caught off guard. It made his pale sweating face all the more worrisome to the viewers at home as he shuffled papers at the podium, looking lost.

"Mr. Governor..."

"Ah, yes, thank you," the Governor said, clearing his throat as he made eye contact with the camera. **"To all the people of our great state, we ask you to be strong. We have**

suffered an attack by unknown parties, for unknown reasons. What we do know is that we will prevail. For everyone's safety, we have declared a state of emergency. Everyone should remain inside behind locked doors until further notice. A strict curfew is being enforced as of now. Please stay off the roads and safely inside so we can regain control of the situation. We are working to call up the national guard. Please stay safe."

There were no questions. The Governor finished his prepared statement and stood, staring at the camera until the regular news channel came back on.

"I keep waiting for some good news," Rylie said.

"I do too," Parker said heavily.

Parker and Riley stayed glued to the news channels, waiting, hoping in vain, for the tone to change. They learned a few minutes after the emergency broadcast that downtown had been declared a no-fly zone. News helicopters showed long distance shots of fires or masses of people moving down streets from so far away it was impossible to see individuals. The Governor's office wanted to keep the airspace free for military and medical use.

The no-fly zone changed the tempo of the broadcasts. Ground crews found their footage in high demand now that the helicopter feeds were essentially worthless. From the sky outside the no-fly zone, every street looked pretty much the same. Ground crews began to share shots of police barricades and people being dragged out of cars and put into handcuffs. The police were taking the curfew seriously. It only made the situation worse. Police struggled with the masses of people trying to get away from the heart of the city while others were trying to get in, determined to find their loved ones. A red circle had been drawn around the heart of the downtown area. A quarantine zone had been created.

"How far are we from downtown?" Rylie asked timidly as they watched a checkpoint firing on a mass of people trying to move down the street.

"Not far enough. They showed a barricade off the 805 which puts us less than a mile outside their restricted zone," Parker said, her lips pursed as she focused on the TV.

A half hour later they watched in horror as the San Diego Nightly news showed one of their anchors being trampled by a mob. A horde of bodies turned the corner as the crew was filming a mixed group of police, troopers, and what looked like national guardsmen trying to set up a barricade using fire trucks and police vehicles. The horde swept into view from a side street and then the camera was on the ground recording a stream of shuffling feet as people screamed amid the rapid pop, pop, pop, of gunfire.

"I need to make a call," Parker said after the shaken team in the news room announced they had been unable to reach their team on the ground since the incident. The next time they showed the map of the restricted zone it had grown. Everything from downtown to the water was now off limits. The quarantine zone was slowly growing. Parker muted the TV and grabbed her phone.

"Maybe we should just go," Rylie said, watching Parker's phone with worry as it powered on. What was Parker doing?

"I'm going to call an old friend. He owes me. I just need to find out what's happening from someone not in the media," Parker said.

"Is he a cop?" Rylie asked.

"Yes," Parker said, her eyebrows raising in question.

"Is it safe? Someone told the Killer I cut my hair," Rylie said, staring at the couch between them, not sure how Parker would react to being questioned.

"I think we have bigger problems now," Parker said, "but even so, I kept his daughter off the books when I found her at a gang bangers house after a homicide. She was so high she had no idea what was going on. He's old school and knows the score between us," Parker said.

Rylie nodded, she had no choice but to trust Parker's judgement.

Parker stood up, waiting impatiently as her phone connected to the cell network. There was a long pause after Parker dialed the number before the phone rang. Rylie sat on the couch, chewing her fingernails as the phone rang once, then twice. Rylie heard the gruff voice pick on up on the other side but couldn't understand what he was saying. She continued to bite her nails as Parker talked to her friend. Rylie listened to Parker's side of the conversation eagerly, wanting to curse at Parker for not putting the damn phone on speaker.

"It's that bad?" Parker said. She listened for a while and then swallowed. "Maybe you should go get her and leave now," Parker said, then paused as the person on the other side spoke. "No, I understand," she said, flexing her free hand and then clenching it into a fist repeatedly as she listened. "I appreciate that Frank, I know you mean it. Can you ring me when you pick

Judith up?" There was a short pause, "I promise we'll be ready. All you will need to do is stop and we'll jump in."

Rylie waited as long as she could after Parker hung up the phone, doing her best to let Parker regain her composure. Parker looked shaken by whatever Frank had told her. "What did he say?" Rylie blurted out when she couldn't take it any longer.

"He's not going to work tomorrow. His wife is a pediatric nurse and they are evacuating her hospital. As soon as her shift ends or the kids are out he is going to pick her up, then us, and we are all getting out of town." Parker nodded her head as she spoke, agreeing with herself, or maybe trying to convince herself it was the best course of action.

"We could leave now," Rylie suggested again, trying to keep the fear out of her voice.

"They've quarantined the city, or at least shut down the highways. Frank's Jeep is a rock crawler. He can go places no one else would even think about," Parker said. "I think it's worth waiting for him." She set her phone down and ran her fingers through her hair.

"I guess we wait then," Rylie said with a heavy sigh, sinking back into the couch cushions.

Parker eventually sat back down and unmuted the news. Half the stations were now running static emergency images telling everyone to stay inside and off the roads. The other stations were full of pundits interspersed with a few frightening interviews. The riots were continuing to grow. The police were being overrun and the National Guard call up was happening more slowly than pre-emergency planning would have predicted.

Rylie watched until she couldn't take it any longer. She fled to the bathroom and splashed cold water on her face before looking down at herself. Her jeans were stained with blood. She had the Red Summer Killer's blood on her. Looking at the blood on her pants made her stomach turn over and she had to clamp her mouth shut to keep from throwing up.

Rylie felt soiled. She took a deep breath and centered herself before going back out into the bedroom and poking her head into the living room. "I need to take a shower; do you care if I borrow some more clothes?" she asked.

"There are jeans and shorts in my duffel and other clothes in the bedroom. Take whatever you need," Parker said, barely paying attention to her. She was focused on whatever new horror the TV was sharing.

Rylie grabbed a pair of cotton shorts from Parker's duffel and went into the bathroom, stripping off her clothes as quickly as she could while trying not to touch any of the blood stains. She stuffed everything into the bathroom trash can the best she could and then pushed it into the corner under the sink. She showered quickly, scrubbing down and rinsing off as fast as she could. She dried herself and pulled on the shorts she'd pulled from Parker's bag. The shorts were loose on her. She didn't care, they were clean. She threw a towel around her shoulders and walked back out into the bedroom to find a shirt. She looked in a few drawers before giving up and opening the closet.

"Who puts tee shirts on hangers?" Rylie mumbled to herself as she looked at the neatly arranged clothing hanging in front of her.

"My ex has some serious obsessive-compulsive issues," Parker said, reaching around Rylie to grab a yellow shirt with a number on its back. Rylie jumped, she'd been so lost in thought she hadn't heard Parker slip in behind her. She stepped back and hugged the towel to her chest as Parker held the shirt up to judge its size on Rylie.

"Oh, I'm so sorry," Parker said quickly, realizing that Rylie was looking at her in surprised discomfort. She turned her body back towards the door as she held the tee out behind her for Rylie to take.

"Hmm, thank you", Rylie said weakly, taking the shirt, not sure what to say. "You didn't do anything wrong, I'm just not used to this," Rylie said, grabbing the tee and pulling it on.

"Don't be sorry, just let me know if I cross into your personal boundaries and don't realize it," Parker said, pulling the bedroom door shut as she slipped back into the living room. Rylie had to stifle a mad giggle. The world was tearing itself apart outside and yet she was still reacting as if being caught wearing a towel was something to worry about.

Parker was sitting on the couch when Rylie made her way out of the bedroom, the television off, a serious look on her face. Rylie walked around the coffee table in front of the couch and sat down on the opposite end of the couch, mildly wary. How bad was the news? Parker looked both serious and worried. Rylie fidgeted on her end of the couch, growing more fearful as Parker sat there, clearly trying to start a conversation she wasn't sure how to begin.

"Did someone hurt you? Did something happen at Ten Acres before you ran?" Parker asked quickly, her words soft, her eyes locking with Rylie's, her expression a mix of worried understanding. No matter what was happening outside the apartment, Parker was still a cop.

"Not…" Rylie struggled, she was not used to talking to anyone about herself, "…not like that. The thing with the counselor happened because I refused to let him make me his girlfriend. I stabbed him with the only thing I had."

"A pencil," Parker said. "You know it's not your fault if anything happened, the streets can be a tough place to survive," Parker said, her voice remaining soft and calm as she stared at Rylie. Rylie wondered how many times Parker had said something similar to other girls as a police officer, but she also saw something there which was unmistakable. Parker wasn't just asking because she was a cop, Parker was asking because she cared. Rylie met Parker's stare and almost started to cry. "It's okay," Parker promised.

"I was lucky," Rylie said, swallowing back the lump of emotions in her throat. "I wasn't abused, I'm just not used to having anyone close to me," Rylie said, unable to keep a few tears from spilling from her eyes. The words made her think of Donna. "It's been a rough night," Rylie said, wiping tears away with her hands. "Thank you for being here, for caring," Rylie spit the words out quickly. She was not used to having someone put themselves out there for her, and it was both scary and wonderful all at the same time.

"It's okay," Parker promised, putting her hand out, palm up on the space between the two of them.

Rylie looked at Parker's hand, suddenly afraid. She was the lone wolf. She survived by not needing anyone. Rylie lifted her hand and held it over Parker's. All she need to do was let her hand fall. Fear and exhilaration blended into a stream of confusing emotions. Rylie's first instinct was to shut down, to put up her emotional shields. Her hand trembled in the air. Rylie looked at Parker, at the way Parker patiently waited, giving her the time to make her decision. Rylie could feel her future teetering in front of her, not because she feared Parker would reject her if she didn't take her hand, but because she realized that she was stronger with Parker, than without.

Rylie let her hand fall into Parker's gently. She was afraid, then excited as Parker's hand closed around hers, warm, soft, and yet strong all at the same time. Rylie's hand grasped Parker's back fiercely. Fresh tears rolled down her cheeks. Tears of relief. Tears of joy.

"I'm sorry," Rylie said with a smile, her voice thick.

"You're an incredibly tough person Rylie. There is no shame in a few well-deserved tears," Parker said softly. "It's been a long day, you should get some sleep while you can, as soon as Frank's wife walks out of the hospital we'll be rolling," Parker said, her voice trailing off as the sound of helicopters flew by overhead, drowning her out.

"I don't know if I'm going to be able to sleep," Rylie said honestly.

"I'm sure you feel that way now, but once you get under the covers you'll realize how tired you are," Parker promised, standing up to pull Rylie into the bedroom.

Rylie didn't want to let go of Parker's hand, but she had to in order to climb into bed. Parker pulled the blankets up around Rylie's shoulders and told her goodnight. Parker was right. As soon as Rylie snuggled down into the covers the exhaustion won out over everything else and her eyes grew heavy. Rylie watched, half awake, as Parker rooted in the closet for a minute, found what she was looking for, and then slipped out of the bedroom, turning off the light as she left.

Rylie fell asleep feeling safe because she knew Parker was in the next room over.

Chapter 10

"Uhh," Rylie moaned as Parker opened the bathroom door, flooding the bedroom in a swath of light.

"Sorry," Parker whispered, shutting the bathroom door enough that the light wasn't right in Rylie's face. Rylie opened her eyes to slits, watching Parker put a few things from the dresser into a backpack before setting it down by the bathroom door, next to the shotgun. Rylie wondered how long Parker had been packing while she slept. Rylie grunted something that might have been a thanks when Parker turned off the bathroom light. She was so tired she didn't even complain when Parker climbed into bed next to her.

All Rylie wanted to do was go back to sleep.

Rylie woke up feeling warm and cozy. It took her a moment to remember where she was. Parker was behind her, the detective's arm thrown sleepily across her hip. Rylie wondered if this was the sort of thing that girls did when they had sleepovers. She was surprised to find that It actually felt nice to have someone she liked and trusted so close to her.

Rylie lay there enjoying the quiet, half asleep and half awake; at least until Parker's cell phone rang at the same time it vibrated across the nightstand on Parker's side of the bed. Parker rolled over with a grunt and grabbed the phone, answering it with a sleep filled voice. "We'll be ready Frank, 22C, Garden Avenue, yes, that's the place, we are above the art store, in the back," Parker said, rolling out of bed. She slapped Rylie's legs as she walked around the end of the bed to grab the pants and shoes she'd laid out for herself.

"Time to go, Frank will be here in less than five and he's not going to wait for us. He sounds scared," Parker said.

"Got it," Rylie said, throwing the covers off and going to the dresser where Parker handed her a pair of jeans. Rylie pulled the jeans on and went into the bathroom to find her shoes.

Rylie jumped when the first fist falls hit the front door. Frank must have been very close when he called. Rylie heard Parker speaking as she pulled on her shoes and tied them. "You look like shit Frank," Parker said, the words muffled by the distance between the bathroom and the front door.

The loud crash that came next made Rylie jump, her eyes wide with surprise. She cocked her head, waiting for another sound, goosebumps rising along her neck as she stood, listening. Within five seconds of the crash there was a muted scream from Parker followed by another, more muted thud. Rylie darted to the bedroom door and peaked out just in time to see Parker skidding across the living room floor on her butt. Parker came to a halt in front of the couch, clutching her chest as her face turned red.

Rylie's first instinct was to rush to Parker's side. She had her hand on the door knob and was about to fling it open when another pained sound stopped her. Someone was in the kitchen. Rylie forced herself to take a breath and shifted her position, angling to get a better view of the kitchen.

Two men stepped into view. Frank was middle aged and heavy set, which made it strange to see him hunched down, driven forward by the fingers wrapped around the back of his neck. The younger man had a much leaner build, but he didn't seem to struggle to control Frank. A small pent up breath escaped Rylie, the man in the kitchen wasn't the Red Summer Killer. The relief was short lived. The young man waited long enough for Parker to pull herself to a sitting position by the couch before he held up a ten-inch chef's knife in his right hand, making sure that Parker saw it before ramming it through the back of Frank's chest. The tip blade pushed Frank's shirt out before cutting through it over his left breast. Frank took one last breath as he clutched at the knife spearing his heart, not feeling the way the blade cut into his fingers. The young man pushed Frank's body off the blade with a look of satisfaction on his face.

"Frank," Parker croaked with the half a breath she'd managed to suck into her lungs.

"Calling him was a mistake," the young man told Parker smugly. "With everything else going on, he still called it in."

"Fuck you," Parker hissed, lifting herself to her knees as she drew her sidearm from beneath the overhang of her shirt. Rylie expected to hear the pope, to see Parker rise victorious as she emptied her pistol into Frank's murderer. There was no gunshot though, just a blur of motion. One moment Parker was lifting her pistol and the next the young man was in front of her, kicking the weapon from her hand. The gun flew back, bounced off the two walls in the corner, and fell with a thud at the same time that Parker fell back on her ass.

"Are you the Red Summer Killer?" Parker asked, scrabbling backwards along the couch as she tried to put space between her and her attacker. Rylie already knew the answer. The man wasn't the Killer, he was too compact, too young. Rylie had seen the Killer very clearly at Saint Mary's.

"Yes, and no, let's just say that I work for him," the man

said with a laugh, surprising both Rylie and Parker with his response. The young man's voice was deep and rich, hinting at a strong accent. "Tell me where the girl is," he said, his voice filling the room with authority as he spoke. The voice hummed in Rylie's head, reverberating against her skull in an odd, unpleasant way. It's effect on Parker was vastly different.

The words seemed to hurt Parker. She struggled visibly, her eyebrows knitting together as her face scrunched up in pain. "She ran last night," Parker said, spitting each word out with a little squeak. "She went back to the streets," she blurted, sighing heavily in relief when the words were out.

"Sit," the man commanded, an expectant smile on his face as he pointed at the couch in front of him with the tip of the chef's knife. Rylie felt the same hum in her skull, felt pain behind her eyes like a migraine was forming. She expected Parker to curse at her assailant. She watched in amazement as Parker crawled to the couch and climbed into a sitting position. Parker blinked and looked around, seemingly just as surprised as Rylie that she'd done what she'd been told. Rylie expected Parker to surge forward, to attack, but Parker's rear remained firmly on the couch cushion.

"Your hand," the man said, pulling the end table up to Parker's knees. He grabbed her hand and held it to the table as he brandished the chef's knife in front of her. "My master pulled this from his leg and he wanted to make sure the little bitch paid the price for what she did," he said, resting the top third of the knife on the table while placing the wide base of the blade directly over Parker's pinky finger.

"I'm not that gifted, but I can tell by the way you struggle that you're lying," the man said.

"Tell me where the girl is?" he commanded again, his voice changing, his words deepening. Rylie felt his command as if it were a physical thing between her ears. She was aware of it, and it was odd and painful, but the effect it had on Parker was profound. She writhed on the couch in an odd squirming motion, her upper body trying to escape her captors grasp while her rear end barely moved on the couch. The grip Parker's captor had on her wrist never faltered, he kept her hand pinned to the table.

"She ran," Parker screamed, spit flying off her lips.

"I'm glad you're a fighter," the man said, his accent coming through more heavily as excitement filled his voice. Parker screamed into his face in rage, her legs propelling her upright until the young man slammed his forehead into hers, driving her back down into the couch, all the while never letting go of her left hand. "Sit down," he commanded again, the word deep and heavy, settling on top of Parker. She arched her back, her face turned to the ceiling as she howled, trying to fight the physical and mental hold he had on her.

"Where is the girl?" he commanded again, his voice now full of venom. Parker spit at him.

The tone of Parker's scream changed as the knife came down on her flesh, her voice going shrill and high as the blade cut through skin and bone, separating her left pinky finger from her hand with a snick as the blade came to rest on the end table. The young man shifted Parker's severed finger away from the rest of her hand with a flick of the knife as he watched the blood pooling around her hand with a hungry look. He lifted the knife and set it above her left ring finger as Parker sobbed. "Where is the girl?" he repeated, licking his lips, his breathing picking up as he grew more excited.

Parker's face was bright red, her lips trembling as she spoke. "She," Parker whimpered, each word an effort to get out. "She took the shotgun and ran," Parker said very carefully, glaring angrily at the man about to cut off another of her fingers.

"Where?" the man commanded as Rylie stepped away from the door and spun about. The bag and the shotgun were leaning next to the dresser. She darted to the shotgun and picked it up. Parker was giving her what help she could, prodding Rylie to do what she couldn't.

"She's hiding in the bedroom," Parker screamed, her voice cracking as she gave in to the young man's demand. She'd fought has hard as she could. She didn't understand what she was fighting, but she'd fought none the less.

Rylie darted to the shotgun, her hands grabbing it and pulling it to her as she spun around just in time to see the door between the bedroom and the living room being pushed open. Parker screamed Rylie's name from the couch. She wanted to get up, to help, but she couldn't seem to move her legs.

"Don't move," the young man commanded them both; his voice full of satisfaction. He'd found his target. Rylie pulled the shotgun up to her shoulder, ignoring the painful buzz between her eyes as her finger searched for the safety and pushed it in. Rylie heard Parker's voice in her head, telling her to put the bead at the end of the shotgun in the middle of the circle.

"So, you were here the whole time," the man spoke, showing no sign of fear as he looked at Rylie. "Put the weapon down," he commanded. Rylie imagined she could feel the words moving through the air, distorting it in ripples that hit her with physical force. The words were like unwanted hands trying to touch her, to force her to move, to obey. She shivered as the feeling fluttered cross her skin. Her attacker saw her reaction, his expression changing. His confidence faltered, replaced with a flicker of doubt that reached his eyes just as he began to move.

Rylie pulled the trigger, yelping as the recoil rammed the butt of the shotgun back into her shoulder. No one heard her yelp, the sound of the shotgun in the confined spaced blotted out all other noise. The recoil pushed Rylie backwards as the room lit up and the sound of the blast echoed in her ears. She took one fumbling step backwards before her back hit the wall next to the bathroom door, keeping her upright. She pushed forward, balancing on her now rubbery legs, pulling the shotgun back up to her shoulder, looking at the man she'd just shot at down the barrel of the shotgun, not sure if she'd hit him.

He was still on his feet. Swaying slightly from side to side, looking back at Rylie with a look of surprise. His eyes were wide, his mouth hanging open as the color drained from his face. Their eyes locked and his focus narrowed on her. He gritted his teeth, his color rising as anger and hate filled him. Their eyes broke contact as pain made him grimace and he shifted his gaze downward to where his hands were clutching his abdomen. Because he was wearing a dark shirt it was hard to see the wound in his gut, but the blood running down his legs was already soaking into the carpet, turning it a dark red. The knife he'd been holding was now laying forgotten at his feet.

"Put the weapon down," he struggled to say, his brows knitting in concentration.

"No," Rylie whispered back hoarsely. Her voice had fled her.

His lip quivered into a snarl. "Put the weapon down," he commanded, shifting his upper body with a pained grimace as he dragged his right foot forward through the carpet. Even injured he was trying to advance. His feet moved slowly, inching forward one at a time. "Stop," he growled, his voice booming as he put everything he had into the command.

The sound hit Rylie like a physical thing. She felt oddly detached, as if she was watching something that didn't involve her. She stood, not believing that her assailant was still standing under his own power as he crept forward. With each step his gate grew longer, leaving a trail of blood smeared into the rug behind him as he crossed the space between them.

Rylie kept waiting for him to drop. How was he still standing? The thought stuck in her brain, swirling about, looking for an answer. She blinked and the space between them was gone. How had he gotten so close? He was right in front of her.

Terror made her knees weak. If she'd had any fluid in her bladder it would have run down her legs. Her blood pressure spiked, making the wound on the back of her head pulse with each heartbeat.

The fear returned her will to her.

Rylie's hands shook as she worked the pump, pulling it back, concentrating on the sound of the weapon as her attacker commanded her once again. "Stop," he intoned, his voice rough and angry, the words half slurred as he struggled against the pain of the slug which had already torn through his belly. Rylie felt the command, felt the pressure of his word on her skull. He wanted her to obey. A part of her wanted to make him happy, to do what she was commanded to do. Instead she concentrated on the weapon, jamming the pump forward as he lifted his hand out to reach for her, his fingers covered in his own blood.

Panic and fear were twisting Rylie's reality. She imagined his fingernails had grown to inch long claws, dripping blood. He snarled at her and lunged, desperate to close the last few inches between his outstretched hand and her flesh.

Time slowed.

"S-t-o," he began, his mouth opening in slow motion. His eyes locked on hers, drawing her in. His irises had turned to pools of swirling liquid metal. She could feel his command, feel how easy it would be to just do what he wanted.

She ignored those feelings and pulled the trigger.

The tip of the shotgun turned into a jet of fire. Rylie felt the recoil, rejoicing at the way it pushed her back into the wall, putting her a few inches further from his reaching hand. Blood sprayed out behind her attacker as the slug punched through him. He was still moving though, his lunge turning into a stumble. Rylie screamed and sidestepped, jumping up onto the bed to get out of the way as his body slammed into the wall where she'd just been.

His head punched a hole in the drywall then popped free as his body collapsed in a gangly pile. Rylie took two bouncy steps and jumped off the bed. Fear made her turn when she reached the door, half expecting to see him standing again. He wasn't. She sighed in relief. His body was jumbled in a pile, leaning against the wall.

His blood was everywhere. It flowed from him in thick

streams.

"Fuck no," Rylie said as his left hand twitched. She repeated the curse as his fingers crawled across the carpet and dug in. The muscles in his arm bulged slightly as he pulled his body away from the wall until his head fell onto the rug. His legs were bent at odd angles behind him as he struggled to turn his body around using just the strength in one arm.

She couldn't understand how he was still moving. She could see his spine through his back - and yet he was reaching out with his hand, pulling himself around. How was he still alive? Rylie was shaking. He had to be dead. No one could survive those wounds. "Stop," she screamed, begging him to be still. His only reply was to let his fingers crawl across the floor before finding a new grip on the rug. The rest of his body twitched and jerked as he used his left arm to pull himself along, leaving a massive red stain behind him that was thicker where he stopped to find a new grip. Rylie watched in stunned horror as he continued moving, refusing to die.

Rylie screamed when a hand fell on her shoulder. She was trying to spin and get the shotgun pointed in the right direction when she realized it was Parker. Rylie's first reaction was to curse, angry at being scared, which was rapidly followed by relief that Parker was next to her. The look on Parker's face turned that relief to worry. Parker looked haunted. Her face was pale white, and she was staring at the thing on the bedroom floor with shocked disgust as it continued its struggle to close the distance. Parker leaned on Rylie as she lifted her pistol, aiming carefully.

Rylie barely jumped when Parker pulled the trigger. The

handgun sounded like a toy compared to the shotgun.

The man on the floor jerked once as the top of his head popped, spreading blood, bone and pulverized brains onto the floor. His body shook and quivered and very slowly his hand released its grip on the carpet. Rylie watched that fist, holding her breath, afraid it was going to begin to move again. Parker didn't seem to have the same concern. She holstered her pistol and let go of Rylie to stumble back into the living room. Rylie turned to follow her just in time to see her lean over the edge of the couch and throw up.

"Rylie," Parker said, wiping her mouth with her hand and flicking it away. "My keys are by the sink. I need you to get the orange box from the trunk of my car. It looks like a tackle box," she said, using the bottom of her shirt to staunch the blood flowing from her severed finger.

"Be careful," Parker called out as Rylie edged around Frank's body and looked out the shattered apartment door, gripping the shotgun so hard her hands hurt.

A very large black Jeep sat at the bottom of the stairs, blocking most of the alley. Rylie held the shotgun at her side, holding it low but pointed at the Jeep as she made her way down the stairs. She held the weapon steady on the driver's side window until she was low enough on the stairs to see into the vehicle. The Jeep was empty. Off in the distance she could hear sirens, gunfire, and the buzzing of helicopters. She ran down the last few steps and kicked the trash cans away from the rear of Parker's cruiser so she could get to the trunk. She grabbed the orange first aid kit and ran back up the stairs as fast as her legs would carry her.

"It's me," Rylie yelled as she came in, not wanting to get shot by accident.

"Good girl," Parker said, smiling through a sheen of sweat. She was sitting on the couch, bent over her wounded hand as she tried to put pressure on it. "Open the box, in the bottom you'll see foil bags about the size of an instant oatmeal package. Good, good," she said as Rylie held one up for her to see. "Rip it open and poor it over my finger," she said, putting her hand up, looking away. Rylie would have preferred not to look at it either. There was a tiny stub of her pinky left, and Rylie could see the white of bone through the blood.

She tore open the packet and poured it over her finger.

"Fuck," Parker screamed, her good hand clamping down around her wrist. She stomped her foot on the floor as her face turned blotchy red. Rylie looked at the package in her hand, then at Parker, afraid she'd just killed her.

"Are you okay?" Rylie begged as Parker shut her mouth, her jaws bulging. It was a long moment before Parker's jaw muscles unknotted, even then she continued to breath in panting breaths, trying to control the pain.

"That stung like a motherfucker," Parker said between breaths when the worst of it was over. The powder had formed a deep purple coating around her finger and the bleeding had stopped. "Now get some gauze and tape. We need to get out of here," she said, holding her wounded hand by its wrist as Rylie tentatively put a piece of gauze over the stub of her finger and taped it from the back of her hand to the front before wrapping another loop around her fist to hold everything in place. It wasn't pretty, but Rylie figured it would hold.

"We need to get out of here. Go grab the pack," Parker said, nodding to the bedroom. It was the last place Rylie wanted to go. She was glad to see the dead guy on the floor hadn't moved any further. Rylie used the bed to get around the body and grab the pack without putting her feet in any of his blood. She considered it a victory.

Parker was waiting for her in the kitchen when she returned. She was standing by Frank's body. "I'm sorry if I got you killed," she said solemnly before she knelt down. Rylie thought she was going to say a prayer or something. Instead Parker rifled through his pockets. "No keys," she muttered before standing up and moving to the door.

Parker led the way down to the street and checked the Jeep. The keys were in the ignition. Rylie helped push Parker up into the driver's seat before running around to the passenger side and using one of the wheels and a hand grip to climb in herself. She stuffed their pack and the shotgun in the backseat as Parker buckled herself in with one hand.

The Jeep rumbled to life when Parker turned the key before settling into a dull roar that Rylie hoped was normal.

It was time to get out of San Diego.